HER ROYAL BODYGUARD

BOOK 4: HER ROYAL FAMILY

MARGAUX FOX

1

———

"I pronounce you henceforth, Princess Alexandra, Princess of Scotland and Duchess of Fife." The King coughed and nodded at Alex. Alex was stunning in a tartan dress that had been made specially in the Royal Tartan for this occasion. It was sleek around her body and long sleeved, exposing her delicate collarbone and the cleavage of her breasts, and it flowed out from the waist in a full skirt to the floor. The press had gone mad for it. Alex had told Erin at length how she had always loved the summers of her childhood that were spent in the Scottish Highlands at the Royal Family's Scottish castle. She said that was why her father had chosen Scottish titles for her to be given upon her marriage.

Alex and Erin were both happy with the selection. Alex believed passionately in the Scottish government and their strongly feminist approach. Scotland led England in that respect and it was something that Erin knew Alex would try to change in England. England needed more gender equality in many respects, and Erin didn't doubt for a second that, as with anything else that Alex went after, she would achieve change.

The King looked to Erin and coughed again, clearing his throat. "I pronounce you, Sergeant Erin Kennedy to henceforth be known as Sergeant Erin Kennedy, Princess of Scotland and Duke of Fife."

Erin felt overwhelmed by the moment. At no time had she imagined becoming a princess herself, but Alex had warned her that titles would inevitably follow their marriage as was tradition of the monarchy. The "Dukedoms" that the King could give were normally reserved for male members of the Royal Family, but here, the King had made exception, to give the Dukedom of Fife to the wife of his only daughter. Erin had agreed she was happier to be Duke and Alex to be Duchess, and that was how the titles had been given.

Erin hadn't mentioned it to Alex, but she felt as she looked at the King and bowed to graciously accept her new titles that he was putting things in place. Erin sensed a certain finality about him, a man that perhaps didn't see many years left for himself and knew his daughter would be the next monarch on his death. Erin thought it seemed as though he was trying to create an easier path for Alex.

If he gave the titles to Erin, it meant his blessing for them both, which as the first same-sex couple in the Royal family, they were both eternally grateful for.

Alex would never back down from her responsibility as the heir to the throne. Alex had been prepared her whole life for her role as Queen and as with everything else she did, Erin knew that Alex would be an exceptional Queen. Alex was not someone who did things by halves.

∼

THEY MADE it home from the ceremony in the dark and Audrey was delighted to see them.

"You big, spoilt mutt, don't try and pretend you have been all alone while we were out. We all know you haven't." Erin bent down and kissed Audrey's big head and Audrey rubbed against her delightedly.

Alex announced immediately, "Let's honeymoon in Scotland. I adore it there. Honestly. We can go to Caribbean islands and on beach holidays anytime in the future, but let me show you Scotland. My Scotland. The best days of my childhood were spent there. When I was home from boarding school, we always were allowed to spend the summer holidays in Scotland. I know we have to go for official reasons anyway, but let's take some real time away and spend it there."

Erin, as usual, got caught up in Alex's excitement. "I'd love to. There is nowhere in the world I would rather go than to Scotland with you."

Erin had been to Scotland before and it had rained a lot. She had stayed in an overpriced Airbnb in Edinburgh. She had no doubt that going to Scotland as the new Princess of Scotland, alongside Her Royal Highness, Princess Alexandra, to stay in a royal castle in the Highlands would be an entirely different experience.

Shimmer was unfortunately suffering from a minor injury, so it would be a good time to get away. There would be no competitions for Erin and Shimmer for the next few weeks anyway.

Alex caught Erin's eye and suddenly her look was flirtatious. She still wore the stunning tartan dress that looked like it was from another time. She looked like a princess from a castle in the old days. It still amazed Erin every day that Princess Alexandra was hers. Alex had pulled the pins from her hair and her hair glowed golden around her shoulders. "So, Princess Erin, Princess of Scotland, Duke of Fife, why don't you sit down and I will fix you a drink. I'll be your maid. Seeing as you are now a noble, you will need a maid."

Erin smiled to herself. She knew exactly what Alex was up to and she was more than happy to play along. Alex had been requesting role play games regularly now, and Erin always enjoyed them.

"Yes, I think the new Princess of Scotland and Duke of Fife definitely needs a drink. Fetch me a beer, Maid."

Erin took a seat in the big armchair in their living area while Alex rushed immediately to their kitchen area where they had a tall drinks fridge that was always fully stocked and Erin watched as she came back into the room quickly with an open bottle of Budweiser on a tray. At this time of the evening, Erin knew they wouldn't be disturbed.

Alex knelt demurely at Erin's feet and offered up the silver tray and the beer to Erin, and Erin gladly took it. She took a cold swig enjoying the cold beer on her tongue. There was nothing else like a cold beer after a long day.

"Would Princess Erin like a foot massage while she drinks her beer?" Alex looked innocently up at Erin through long lashes.

Erin smiled again. "Princess Erin would absolutely love a foot massage. Take my shoes and socks off, Maid."

Erin knew that Alex enjoyed being told what to do. Erin could tell how much this little game was turning Alex on, and she watched as Alex took both of her feet in turn and carefully unlaced and removed her shoe and then rolled each sock off. She knelt immediately before Erin and took Erin's right foot and began to press and massage it with her hands.

Erin leant back in the chair. Foot massage was definitely up there as one of her favourite things to receive. The glass bottle was cold in her hand as she watched Alex working on her foot. She was focussed and careful.

"Put some effort in, Maid. Make sure you do a good job or I will have to get a new maid." Erin noticed a tiny gasp from Alex and knew that she was enjoying it. She felt the pressure of Alex's fingers increase and keep moving on her foot. Then she watched as Alex's head dipped and her lips met the top of Erin's foot. Alex's lips peppered kisses across Erin's foot and then her tongue ran the length of it from her toes to her shin. Erin felt herself getting hugely turned on watching Alex's mouth and tongue at work. The feeling of Alex's lips against her skin was always something that drove her wild.

"That's better, Maid. Much more like it." Erin watched as Alex's clear blue eyes gazed up at her obediently awaiting further instruction. The swell of her breasts rose and fell with her ribcage as she breathed in and out. Erin could watch her like this forever. "I think you should also massage my legs. It has been a long day. I need to relax. In Scotland, the Dukes and Princesses get a much more full-body treatment. Take off my trousers and my underwear."

Erin sat forwards and splayed her legs apart and Alex shuffled forwards between them and her fingers went to undo the fastenings at Erin's waist.

"Um, Princess Erin, could you stand up please, so I could take them off?"

Erin stood, feeling so powerful suddenly with Alex at her feet, and she waited as Alex pulled down her trousers, then came closer to peel down Erin's underwear. She felt the instant electricity of their connection as she felt Alex's fingers under the elastic waistband. She felt Alex's breath on her skin and enjoyed looking down and seeing her face so close to where Erin ultimately wanted it to be. But she could wait longer, she decided, and she sat back down as Alex peeled the underwear down past her knees and off over her feet.

Alex immediately went back to work obediently rubbing her ankle and calf muscle. Alex's fingers felt incredible on her skin, kneading through the muscles, but Erin knew she wanted more.

"Use your mouth, Maid," Erin said as she took another cool drink from her beer. She felt Alex's lips at her skin. Alex's mouth on her shin bone and her tongue running up towards her knee. Erin watched as gooseflesh rushed across her skin from where Alex's lips were dragging up her thigh.

Alex's mouth was kissing her knee, then the other knee, then suddenly her lips were at the inside of Erin's thigh and her hands were pushing Erin's legs apart to allow her access. Erin noticed Alex's breathing quicken. She loved how much Alex got off on these role play games.

Erin made every effort to stay calm and

act disinterested while she drank her beer, as though Alex's work with her mouth and hands was having no effect at all on her when in fact it was absolutely the opposite.

"That's a good maid, pleasuring your master. Maybe I'll keep you after all."

Alex's mouth reached Erin's groin and her tongue ran up the crease of her groin. First on one side and then on the other. Alex's narrow shoulders edged Erin's legs further apart as Alex shuffled forwards on her knees to gain better access.

Suddenly, Alex's mouth was on Erin's labia, kissing one side, then the other. Moving around everywhere but Erin's clitoris, kissing, nibbling, running her tongue around.

Erin was doing her best to stay calm and not respond physically. She took another drink of her beer.

"I think you should give your master an orgasm, Maid," Erin sighed. "If you do a good enough job, maybe I will reward you."

Alex's tongue parted Erin's folds and pushed inside her. Erin could feel her own wetness as Alex's tongue slid inside of her pushing as deep as was possible.

Erin tipped her head back and relaxed into it. She put what was left of her beer down on the table. She felt the wet heat of Alex's mouth envelope her clit and she moaned loudly.

"There's a good maid."

"Is this to Princess Erin's satisfaction?" Alex breathed as she released Erin's clit for a second.

Erin felt cool air on her clit in the sudden absence of Alex's mouth. She wanted to pull Alex's head back between her legs and never let it go.

"Very much so." Erin smiled, taking hold of a handful of silvery blonde hair. "Now, get back to work." She used her hand to draw Alex's face back to her, and she felt Alex's mouth open and her tongue obediently go back to work. Erin felt the slickness of herself against Alex's mouth. She felt Alex's warm mouth and tongue sliding easily as they worked. Erin looked down watching Alex on her knees; her eyes were closed and her beautiful face was deep in concentration serving Erin. The feeling of immense power rushed to Erin's head as she gripped Alex's hair tighter and thrust her hips against Alex's face. It took seconds of grinding on Alex's face before her body went rigid and her orgasm rushed through her. Every part of her body felt utterly alive. Her hand released its grip on Alex's head and she watched as Alex took a breath. The slickness of Erin's pleasure was evident on Alex's face.

"Very good, Maid." Erin looked down at Alex, still on her knees, still exquisite.

"Thank you, Princess Erin. Thank you for letting me serve you." Alex stayed on her knees, her wide blue eyes looking up hopefully.

"Now, I'll give you your reward, Maid." Erin couldn't wait to touch Alex. She could see in her eyes how turned on she was.

"Get on all fours on the coffee table. Pull your dress up around your waist."

"Of course, Master."

Erin took a breath and a drink of her beer as she watched Alex arrange herself on the table as per the instructions. She watched as Alex struggled to get the heavy skirt of her long dress to stay around her waist. She smiled as she saw that Alex had no underwear on.

"Did you go to that ceremony with the whole world watching and receive a title by the King with no underwear on?"

"Um, yes," Alex mumbled. "I like how it feels to wear nothing under a dress."

Erin stood up, smiling to herself. She loved it when Alex did things like this. Alex was still struggling to arrange her skirt. "Very bad girl, Maid. That is very naughty indeed. I cannot believe you didn't ask your master's permission to go out like that."

"Sorry, Master," Alex said quickly, gasping as Erin's left hand was on the skin of her hip while her right hand pushed the heavy dress right up her back.

Alex's ass was completely on display now. Erin felt a bolt of desire rush through her own body. Everything about Alex on all fours on this coffee table was exciting her. She could see a trickle of wetness on Alex's inner thigh.

She raised her hand and slapped Alex's ass and Alex yelped in response. Spanking was a new thing they had been exploring. As usual, Alex was desperate to explore everything. Erin hadn't been so sure how she would feel hitting Alex like this, but quickly she had realised she liked it. She liked how much Alex enjoyed it and that got her off. There was a red handprint on the cheek of Alex's ass.

Erin slapped the other cheek, a little harder. She knew Alex would say if it was too much and she would stop right away. They had had lengthy discussions about this. Erin loved the power play but she never ever wanted to take it too far, despite Alex's pushing. Erin always watched Alex's body carefully. She noticed every tiny reaction in Alex, from the way she was breathing to the sounds she made, to the way her body moved.

Erin hit her again. "You've been very bad, Maid. Next time you will ask for permission if you want to go out without underwear." Erin watched as Alex's breathing quickened. She noticed another trickle of wet escaping between Alex's legs. She hit Alex again and felt the stinging in her own hand. Alex gasped again.

Erin saw the cold beer bottle next to her chair and had an idea. She picked it up and brought it up between Alex's legs. As the glass rim hit Alex's wetness, she nearly jumped off the table.

"Stay still," Erin warned, "or I will take it away."

This time when she brought the bottle to Alex's pussy, she noticed Alex's breathing was regulated, she was trying hard to be calm and she only moved marginally as the cold glass touched her. Erin ran the bottle up and down Alex's wetness noticing her moans increasing.

"You think I should put this bottle inside you, Maid?"

"Please," Alex gasped, her desperation was evident.

Erin slid it up and down once more, teasingly.

"Please, Master. I'll do anything. Please fuck me."

Alex's pleas always did something to Erin. They always filled her with lust. She pushed the neck of the beer bottle into Alex's wetness knowing how cold it would feel inside her. There was still some beer in it too. That would probably end up inside her. Erin's mind went straight to imagining drinking it out of her later.

Alex was moaning and moving herself back and forth on the bottle neck. Her impatience was showing and as much as Erin wanted to take it slowly and make her wait, she also couldn't resist herself.

Erin used her left hand to hold Alex's hip while she fucked her a bit with the bottle and watched as the neck of it disappeared inside of Alex. The sight of Alex's red ass from the spanking was beautiful.

She knew Alex was desperate to orgasm and she also knew she was desperate to feel Alex orgasm. She pulled the bottle out of Alex and replaced it with her fingers. Three fingers pushing downwards against her G spot as her thumb slid against Alex's clit. Erin could feel how swollen and excited Alex was inside. She knew it wouldn't last long now. It was seconds before she felt Alex tighten around her fingers and explode, calling out loudly.

Erin moved quickly to her knees and replaced her hand with her mouth. She took a welcome mouthful of Alex's orgasm mixed with the beer. It was the sweetest taste in the world. She ran her tongue through Alex a few more times, taking every drop that there was. Then she kissed the red on Alex's ass cheeks tenderly before standing up and helping Alex up from the table and into her arms. She kissed her lips gently and then scooped Alex up into her arms.

"Very good, Maid. Very good girl. You want to go to bed now?"

Alex nodded, her face was relaxed and chill now and her blue eyes were always so trusting as she looked up at Erin. Erin wondered often how she got so lucky. Princess Alexandra was her wife.

"Let's go via the shower and get you out of this dress and get the beer cleaned out of you!"

"There is beer in me?!" Alex laughed. "Well, that's a first!"

2

The following morning, Erin and Alex were taking coffee and breakfast on the terrace. They had made themselves bacon and egg sandwiches. Alex knew she had grown up reliant on chefs to cater for her every need and desire at any time of the day or night so it was a novelty that Erin would make food for them. Alex would assist and learn. Not that Alex had ever been naive to her own immense privilege, but seeing it now, that she really didn't even know how to fry an egg, made her embarrassed of the world that she came from.

Erin never professed to be particularly good at cooking, but she did always say she was the best at a bacon and egg sandwich, and Alex couldn't argue with that. Erin always said it all hangs on the bread being the softest and fluffiest, the bacon being the crispiest and the egg being soft, but not too runny.

Erin often said it was important not to get lazy with all the staff that they had at their disposal to do literally everything for them, and it dawned on Alex just how lazy she had become over the years. She had made secret promises to herself to change that. When she and Erin had children, she didn't want to set the example that had been set to her, that everything was done for them by staff.

As she bit into her sandwich, she felt proud. She had done the eggs today and they were perfect. It seemed such a simple thing, but she felt a real and genuine sense of pride over it.

It felt surreal waking up with Erin who suddenly had a lot of titles to her name. It felt strange that the very act of marrying

Erin had dragged her into her world of immense responsibility. Sure, titles were an honour, but they were also a burden and running the fine line balancing honour and burden had been Alex's life's work.

It was early days, but it seemed like Erin was slipping comfortably into her role. Every time now that they appeared together in public, Erin seemed more natural and less awkward. Alex still felt guilty for how much her love demanded of Erin and then relieved when Erin seemed to take it in her stride. Erin was always calm and composed and exuded strength that Alex had clung to when she needed it.

These days, Alex felt stronger in herself. Coming out to the world had made her feel vulnerable. It had literally made her vulnerable to the threats and attacks that had followed. But every day that went past and every storm that they weathered together, Alex felt stronger, as though their love was enough to get them through anything.

The weight of secrets that Alex had carried her whole life was gone from her now. The Royal Wedding had been a massive success, the whole country had been behind them. They were becoming the Royal power couple that Alex had desperately hoped they might but had never quite dared to believe.

Well, now she was beginning to believe, and it was intoxicating in how powerful it felt.

It was a beautiful morning and they had their whole lives ahead of them.

"So, I know we talked about seeing Dr Keller again and arranging to try and get me pregnant?"

Erin looked up and smiled. "Of course. I'm ready whenever you are. You'll make an incredible mum."

Alex felt happiness flood through her. Having Erin's support meant the world to her. She knew Erin loved kids and had always wanted kids, which really helped, because Alex wasn't totally sure herself. Not that she wasn't going to do it, she had always known she would have children—it was a vital royal duty to continue the royal line and produce heirs—but Alex always wondered if she would have chosen to have children otherwise. It felt like such a massive thing, and if she thought too much about it, it was overwhelming. To bring a child into this world and to have the responsibility of both caring for them and teaching them. To hope that you could protect them from the bad things and give them all the good things. Was wanting to have children a selfish desire? For her, it was her duty that she had always known she would have children.

She knew the pressure that was already on her unborn child, a pressure she was so familiar with herself, but she just hoped that the potential child would be able to cope with it. It was so much to put on a child, to be heir to the British throne.

"Can we talk about sperm donors?" Alex felt vulnerable again. Even though this was Erin—strong, supportive Erin—her wife. It would be so straightforward if she could just have Erin's children, but instead, they needed a donor and Alex was struggling in her head with the options.

"Sure," Erin nodded. "What are you thinking?"

"Honestly, I have no idea. It seems such a lottery. We are supposed to choose 50% of the genetics of the future monarch from a catalogue based on their eye and hair colour? I'm really struggling with it. Then there are the issues that might arise if the donor finds out somehow who they donated to."

"Yeah, I thought that too. I know they would have no legal rights, but it could be complicated if the child wants to know about them when they are eighteen. They would have rights to contact the donor, and if the donor is the kind of person who might exploit having a prince or princess as their child that could be really messy. There is another option, you know?" Erin fixed her with her intense gaze. Her dark green eyes could look almost amber in the sunlight. Her dark hair was slicked back. She looked stunning, as usual.

Alex knew really what she was suggesting; she knew they had both thought about it even though this was the first time they were discussing it.

"Nicolas," Erin said the name that Alex

had been avoiding. It seemed obvious to ask Prince Nicolas, but given their history, Alex didn't want to undermine Erin or upset her by suggesting him. If she had a baby with Nicolas, and the public knew, it was possible people would see it as Nicolas and Alex's child and not Erin's.

"I know." Alex looked down at her hands for a second. "I want you to feel like an equal parent of this baby though, Erin. And I'm scared that you wouldn't if Nicolas is the donor."

"I think that Nicolas is the most polite and respectful man I have ever met and I think it is worth discussing this with him. I think it is quite likely he would be entirely reasonable and in no way overstep his role. I think that given who you are and who this baby will become, it makes sense to have a donor like Nicolas. Someone with their own high status and no ulterior motives. And I also know that I will adore this baby and absolutely be its parent. I'm your wife. This baby will be part of you and whenever I look at it, I will see you and how much I love you. I'm not worried about feeling left out because it wouldn't genetically be mine. Look at how much I love that big lazy giant and I'm fairly sure we aren't related by blood." Erin nodded at Audrey who was stretched out snoring in the doorway—as usual she had chosen the most inconvenient place to lie down.

Alex smiled and felt a warmth rush through her. Why had she ever been scared to talk to Erin? Why had she ever doubted Erin or that their love could triumph over anything?

"Shall I ask him to fly over and we can discuss it, the three of us? What do you think about how to do it? Like do it ourselves at home or do IUI in a clinic where the doctor injects it in?"

"Well, I think IUI has higher success rates, but honestly, it is your body so whatever you are most comfortable with."

"I love you," Alex said, and she meant it. The three words didn't seem like nearly enough for the depth of what she felt for Erin.

"I love you too, Mrs Kennedy." Erin took her hand across the table and lifted it to her lips where she kissed it and the sapphire engagement ring and wedding band that shone brightly on her finger.

Alex felt the electricity of Erin's touch and the love of her kisses.

Alex felt like the luckiest woman in the world.

3

Erin was in the stables tending to Shimmer's injured leg. She had been kicked in the field by one of the other horses and had a wound that would take a few weeks at least to heal. Erin was talking through with the head stable girl, Sara, how to best clean and redress the wound while she was away in Scotland and what her return to exercise programme should be. Shimmer also had antibiotics in powder form that were to go in her feed each day. Sara was a conscientious girl, still young, but very keen and capable. She listened intently and Erin had no doubt that Sara would do the best for Shimmer while she was away.

"Bodyguard! Can't believe I didn't catch up with you after your ceremony last night! I believe there are some new titles in order. Congratulations! I'm literally spoilt for choice with nicknames for you now."

Vic leant over Shimmer's stable door. Her blondish-brown ponytail was unsurprisingly messy and she literally had a bit of straw in it.

"Thank you very much," Erin said, happy to see Vic. They had become such firm friends in the past year even though Erin wouldn't have predicted it. When she had first met Vic, she had wondered how on earth someone as wild as Vic had had the discipline to win an Olympic gold. But that was the thing about Vic, what you saw on the surface was far from all there was. There were layers to Vic, perhaps created over the years to hide who she really was and to protect her. She was a very guarded person. Vic was kind and genuine and capable of anything she put her mind to, and Erin loved those qualities about her.

"So, I was wondering... can I come to

Scotland with you? There is a horse dealer up there I want to visit with some exciting young horses. Also, I want to go out in Edinburgh. Also, I hear the Scottish Royal Residence is fucking incredible and I really want to see it."

Erin laughed out loud. "You want to come on our honeymoon with us?" Vic was never shy in asking for exactly what she wanted.

"Well, I mean, I don't exactly see it like that. We would be staying in a fucking massive castle on a fucking massive estate. I could probably have my own wing so you love birds can have all the married honeymoon sex you want without me listening in. Also, I can entertain myself. I'm not going to gatecrash all your outings. What do you think?"

Erin laughed. "Well, I'm not sure this is for just me to decide. Why don't you ask the Princess yourself? Or are you too scared? Is that why you are asking me?"

"Well, you *are* a princess now. So I thought you were fair game, Sergeant Erin Kennedy, Princess of Scotland."

"Ha. That is a technicality. It's Alex's big

Scottish house. If she's happy, I'm happy, but I'm not going to just invite you on our honeymoon!"

"Well, I was thinking, we could take disguises for you two obviously recognisable famous people and we could all go out in Edinburgh? It would be a blast. Edinburgh is amazing!"

Erin dabbed the wound on Shimmer's leg with the salt water she was using to clean it. It looked good, at least. It was so frustrating she had managed to get kicked in the field, but at least the wound looked clean and was in the large muscle towards the top of her back leg. It could have been so much worse. There is so much power in a horse's kick. It could have shattered Shimmer's bone if it had hit just right. Erin shook her head. She didn't want to think about the worst happening.

"Please, pretty please." Vic wasn't giving up.

"Go and ask Alex!"

"Okay, okay, I will!" Vic looked resigned.

"Where did you get to last night, anyway?" Erin asked her. "Have you just got home?" She noticed Vic still had remnants of last night's makeup on her face.

"Oh god, so I had a night of passion with the Duke of Leicester."

"Leicester?" Erin laughed. "Oh god, no way! He is so annoying!"

"Annoying, YES. Handsome and charming. Also, YES." Vic laughed.

"How was it?"

"Oh, fun. A lot of fucking fun. He is painfully upper class though. He thinks I'm wild."

"You *are* wild."

"He asked to take me out on a date, I said absolutely not. I only do bedroom dates."

"There you go, Victoria Grey-Hughes who doesn't do relationships breaking hearts once again."

"Yeah, you know me, no time for that shit. I'll leave the sickly sweet romance to you and the Princess."

Vic laughed and let herself in the stable door bending to take a look at Shimmer's wound.

"Her wound looks clean and no signs of infection. She can take a break over these few weeks. You probably both need it. Then we can get back to work when *we* are home from Scotty-Mc-Tavish-Land. Might get a couple of runs in before the end of the season, but whether we do or we don't, no matter. You two are going to nail it next season. The national championships has your name all over it. Well, definitely Shimmer's name. Time will tell if you can do her justice as a rider!" Vic looked at Erin suspiciously, as though her dedication and/or aptitude may well be in doubt, even though they both knew it wasn't.

"We will fucking smash next season, Bodyguard. I can feel it in my bones. Let's enjoy this trip to Mc-Tavish-Land and take a well-earned break."

Vic turned and wandered off, while Sara and Erin got back to work re-dressing Shimmer's wound. "Make sure you ask Alexandra!" Erin called loudly.

"Yeah, yeah..." Vic called back in typical Vic fashion. Erin knew damn well she would have to talk to Alex herself and that Vic had no intention of doing so.

∾

THAT EVENING ALEX and Erin were home together. Erin was teaching Alex how to make a stir-fry for dinner. Erin knew her own cookery skills were very limited, but she could at least prepare basic meals. She had never known someone with absolutely zero knowledge of how to prepare food as Alex. Erin knew that Alex was embarrassed by it, so she never made a big deal out of it. She just taught her as though she were a child. It was nice to cook together some-times when they had time. Obviously, it was so much easier and better when they asked the chefs to prepare meals for them, but there was something very satisfying about doing it themselves.

Alex had been tasked with chopping veggies and Erin was fascinated by the look of intense concentration on her face while she focussed entirely on the mushrooms in front of her and the big knife in her hand.

"So, she probably hasn't bothered asking you herself even though I told her she had to, but Victoria Grey-Hughes wants to come to Scotland with us." Erin decided the Vic thing needed dealing with.

"On our honeymoon?" Alex laughed.

"That is *so* Vic."

"Well, she says she wants to visit a horse dealer up there. She promises to keep to her own wing in the big, posh Scottish residence."

"Well, I don't mind. She is easy to have around and we can definitely do our own thing. Also, I spoke to Nicolas and he is going to fly into Edinburgh and meet us up there. So, if Nicolas is going to be there for a bit, there is no real harm in Vic being there for a bit. What do you think?"

"I'm easy. Honestly. As long as we get time together, it might be nice having the others around for some of it. She wants us to go on a night out in Edinburgh in disguise."

Alex laughed and put the knife down. "Well, you know I have a great selection of wigs and I *love* a disguise!"

Erin put her arms around her and kissed her. "Well, you had better pack a wig for me because apparently I also need disguising these days—now that I am married to the most famous princess in the world."

Alex laughed again and Erin felt luckier than anyone else in the world.

4

Alex had always loved Scotland. As a child she had spent her summers there in the Royal Residence, which was a huge country estate and castle, not dissimilar to the one she lived in now outside of London with Erin. Arriving in Scotland for the last few weeks of British Summertime was something that excited her. She couldn't wait to show Erin around *her* Scotland and she realised in that moment that she wanted to do it every year. She wanted to get back to spending her summers in the wilds of North Scotland.

There was something very freeing about being up in Scotland where there were no people. There were the striking mountains and endless moorland and heather and rocks and lochs. It was beautiful up there, and Alex at times could feel like she was just Alex. She could let go of being a princess and just be herself, and for her they were always the happiest moments.

It was raining when they arrived at the castle late at night a few weeks later. A light warm summer rain. Vic was visiting a horse dealer on the border of England and Scotland, and she would head up the following day, so there was just Alex and Erin and their security team that arrived at the castle. Other staff had been sent on ahead.

It was nearly midnight, but Alex felt utterly alive as they got out of the car.

Scotland this far north in the summer never got dark. Not properly. There was an eerie light to it through the rain.

"Why isn't it dark?" Erin asked, looking surprised.

"It never really is in the summer here.

We are far enough north, you see. I always loved that about being up here. It is like another world, isn't it? Like it is never really nighttime, it is always kind of daytime."

Alex watched as Erin stared up at the sky. There were clouds and rain, but beyond that there were the stars in the dim light and they were beautiful.

"It's like nothing I have ever seen before. I mean, I understand the science why it doesn't get dark at night, but I'm just so used to darkness at nighttime, I can't even comprehend this in reality. It is so weird. It's so silent up here too. Like we've driven so far away from everything."

"I know." Alex took Erin's hand and squeezed it. "That is another thing I love here. I can be just me. We are so far away from reality, I feel free."

They both sat on the steps to the castle in the light rain watching the sky. Alex wasn't bothered by it. Alex noticed the security team moving past them into the castle and the drivers heading off to park the cars, and they were suddenly left in peace.

"Want to come out with me and see one of my favourite places in the world?"

"Now?"

"Yes. If you aren't too tired."

"Funny, I don't feel tired at all. Sure."

"Okay, five minutes. Let me go and explain to security what we are doing, then we will head out."

ALEX HAD INFORMED security where they were going. She didn't expect any trouble up here and she knew it was an easier location for the security team to protect, being so isolated. She knew the cars would follow at a distance and she responsibly wore her tracked silver bracelet and handed Erin her own tracked bracelet to clip onto her wrist. Alex knew people who resented having to take security with them everywhere and did what they could to get out without them. There were definitely times in the past it had frustrated her too. As much as Alex would have loved to have gone out with Erin alone tonight, she knew she could find a way to be with Erin alone but also let security know where she was and be able to track her. She didn't want people panicking and she knew it was important to Erin that they worked with the security team. Since the attack on them that had ended with Erin getting shot, Alex made every effort to work with security. She dreaded to think what might have happened that day if their security team had not acted so quickly. She liked knowing she could press the emergency button on her bracelet and the security team would be there straight away.

Alex walked hand in hand with Erin and there was a real peace as they walked off the estate and into the open.

The strange light somewhere between light and dark showed them silhouettes of the mountains against the sky. Alex watched as Erin took it all in and looked around her.

"It is so incredible. I have never seen anything like it. These rocks, these mountains, this beautiful sky. Alex squeezed her hand. She could hear the sound of water from the little stream she used to play in as a child. She caught sight out of the corner of her eye of a reflection in the strange light. It was the eye of a deer. She stopped and turned to Erin, motioning for quiet with a finger to her lips. She pointed to the deer and watched as Erin's eyes widened in fascination. Alex looked further into the murky light and they both stood still as they watched. There were three red deer ahead of them. A noble stag standing proudly with his antlers high against the sky and two smaller deer that Alex thought were females. They were beautiful. Erin turned to her and smiled. Then they both watched as the deer eyed them suspiciously and then moved off calmly, yet purposefully. This was their home, and Alex as usual felt honoured to be able to explore it.

It had been years since she had ventured out at night like this in the Highlands. It was so much better having someone to go with.

"That was amazing," Erin whispered. "They were so cool. I've never been so close to a wild animal like that."

"There are so many of them out here," Alex whispered back. "It is amazing what you can see out here when you let yourself really look."

They walked further and Erin's hand felt warm and strong in her own. It was still raining lightly, but the evening was so warm it didn't seem to matter. Alex was wearing a light, short summer dress and sandals and Erin had shorts and a T-shirt on. They had dressed casually for travelling, not having to dress to be photographed for once, and it felt good. They rounded a rocky outcrop and even though Alex knew what was around the corner she still felt overwhelmed by the beauty of it, and she heard Erin gasp as she took in the wide expanse of water in front of them. From the mountains to the skyline and beyond.

"So this is the famous loch," Erin whispered. "A big and beautiful lake."

"*Lake* is a banned word in Scotland. We must call it a *loch*."

"A big and beautiful loch," Erin sighed and took it all in. "You were right, it is stunning."

Alex smiled to herself. It was every bit as beautiful as the last time she had been here. She led Erin down to the edge of the water and along the edge to a lovely, shallow beach-like area.

Alex turned to Erin and pulled her dress up over her head. Knowing what she was planning, she had left her underwear at the castle. She stood naked in the half light and looked confidently at her wife. "Take off your clothes. We are going in."

Alex felt Erin's eyes on her body and a jolt of desire ran through her.

Erin laughed. "Are you sure? Is it safe?"

"Absolutely. It is so nice, I promise. I swam in here so many times as a kid."

"Naked?" Erin asked, giving her a look.

"Ha. Sometimes." Alex smirked back as she turned and waded into the water. Then, as it reached her waist, she took a deep breath, plunged in, and began to swim under water. The cold of the water over her head and her whole body hit her with a rush. There was something about wild swimming that always made her feel so alive. Swimming nude had always been a thrill for her. Not that she had done it loads, but she wanted to. Being with Erin gave her the confidence to.

She turned back to shore and swam on the spot laughing.

She watched as Erin stripped off on the little beach area. She never got tired of seeing Erin's body. She liked the way the light fell on her muscles, her strong shoulders and arms and her tight stomach. The neat patch of dark curls between her legs and her muscular thighs. Erin began to wade towards her and Alex noticed her nipples harden with the cold. She smiled to herself. Suddenly Erin plunged in too and swam towards her, grabbing hold of her and pulling her under momentarily. Alex wasn't afraid; she was a confident swimmer and had grown up swimming in this loch. She knew it intimately. She laughed as they both popped their heads up out of the water. Their legs were still paddling and their arms were around each other. Alex felt the heat of Erin's body against her own and they kissed intensely. There was always a magic and ownership to Erin's kiss that ran through Alex's body rendering her defenceless.

But now wasn't about sex. It was about the magic of swimming in the loch in the half light and feeling so close to nature and feeling so free.

"You happy to swim for a bit?" Alex asked as they both took a breath. Erin nodded and their bodies parted. Alex led and she found Erin swimming alongside her, slightly behind. It reminded her of the way Erin used to walk next to her, but slightly behind, when she was her body-guard, before she was her lover and her wife.

Erin would tell her it was the best way to protect her, to be close to her, but still able to see everything. Alex asked Erin once why sometimes she was on her left and sometimes on her right and Erin told her that she always positioned herself on the side of the most likely danger. So if they walked along a pavement, Erin was always positioned between Alex and the traffic. Erin still did it now, instinctively, even though she wasn't Alex's bodyguard any-more, Alex knew she was always protecting her. There was something eternally ro-mantic about that, Alex thought, that Erin was always protecting her.

It hadn't been romantic at all when Erin

got shot with a bullet meant for Alex, though. That had been the most fear Alex had ever felt. The thought that she might lose Erin had been overwhelmingly terrifying. Alex still could see the scars on the back of Erin's ribcage where the bullet had entered her body. If she ever needed it, it was a vivid representation of Erin's devotion and love for her. Any chance Alex got, she would run her mouth over the scars so Erin knew that her devotion to Alex was returned in every way.

Now, Erin swam close to Alex, but between Alex and the shore and Alex knew that was a purposeful decision to protect her from any potential danger on the shore.

But now, here in the amazing water, there was no danger to them. There was just the endless peace and the stars above them and the dark water stretching far ahead of them and the mountains surrounding them and absorbing them into their world.

"This is my favourite place," Alex said as they swam.

"I can see why," Erin said. "It's lucky I can swim."

"Very," Alex said. "I knew you would be able to."

"I actually did my lifeguard qualifications years ago. Which is a good job seeing as we are out here on our own."

"I'm not going to drown, not out here! Don't worry! Although, maybe I should, because I know you get off on saving people." Alex smiled at her wife.

"Has there ever been a sport that you weren't good at?"

"Definitely tennis," Erin laughed.

"Lack of practice," Alex laughed. "You need to play more. We need a fourth person to play now that Annabelle is no more."

They swam a little further in the cool water. Alex felt like her body had adjusted to the temperature now and although it was cool, in keeping moving, her body could tolerate it well.

"How do you feel about Annabelle now after what she did?"

Alex thought for a few seconds before answering. "Confused. Hurt. Angry. I still can barely believe it. For so many years I was so cautious about who I trusted. And rightly so, it seems."

Alex thought about Annabelle, her seductive nature, her great friendship, her betrayal; all the things she loved about her and all the things she hated about her. *That's the thing*, Alex thought as she swam, enjoying the feeling of the water against her naked body, *none of us are all good or all bad*. Annabelle is a prime example of both. Someone whose endless desires for money and status had brought out all the bad in her.

The rain still fell lightly on her face above the water. She felt fresh, renewed and reborn. They swam in near silence for another twenty minutes in a loop around this end of the loch.

"Are there prehistoric monsters in this loch?" Erin asked, lightening the tone.

"No, not this loch. Only in Loch Ness. The Loch Ness Monster. Anyway, I reckon she is friendly," Alex laughed.

They made it back to the little beach uneventfully and as they got out, Alex felt the cold of the water start to get to her. "Okay, we have to run up this hilly bit to warm up. Get ourselves moving to shake off the chill of the loch. I'll race you to that tree." Alex started running from the beach up the hillside, the ground hard and rough under her feet that definitely were no longer used to running around barefoot. She heard Erin laugh and suddenly felt the presence of her closing in behind her, and it thrilled Alex to be chased by her.

Alex gasped as she felt the thud of Erin's body against her own tackling her down onto a patch of springy heather.

She felt the thrill rush through her of Erin on top of her as she lay face down in the heather, her naked wet, cool skin smooth against Alex's own. She felt Erin's hard nipples pushing against her back, and the weight of Erin on top of her felt good.

"Are you okay?" Erin whispered in her ear.

"Yes," Alex heard herself murmur. She felt lust flowing freely through her body and pooling between her legs.

"How safe is this lake water?"

"Loch," Alex corrected. "It is so clean. So natural. We are so far from the dense populations up here the water is safe to drink."

"Good," Erin murmured in her ear. "Because I want to drink you in."

Alex shuddered underneath Erin. Erin's whisper was so intense in her ear. She felt Erin take her earlobe in her mouth and suck it. Erin's mouth felt hot on her cool skin. Alex heard a loud moan and realised it was her own. God, she wanted Erin to take her so badly right now.

The heather felt scratchy on her belly and breasts, but she didn't care. An animalistic need had taken over inside of her and desire to be fucked was all she could feel. She felt herself trying to part her legs under the weight of Erin's body.

"What's that, Mrs. Kennedy? Opening your legs for me?"

Of all her many titles, Alex enjoyed her unofficial *Mrs. Kennedy* title the best. It meant she was Erin's wife, and it thrilled her when Erin called her that.

"Mmm," Alex mumbled.

"What do you want?" Erin asked, running her fingers down Alex's side at the same time as her tongue ran around Alex's ear.

Alex always felt a sudden shyness overcome her when she had to ask for it, and she knew Erin got off on making her squirm.

"I need you to fuck me," Alex whispered into the heather bed that she lay upon. Suddenly she no longer felt cold. Heat was rushing through her from every angle.

"What's that, Mrs. Kennedy? I didn't hear you."

"Please," Alex gasped as Erin took her earlobe in her mouth again. Then her mouth slid to Alex's neck and her tongue glided across Alex's slick skin.

"Tell me what you want, Mrs. Kennedy, or you won't get it."

Alex took a deep breath. The thought of Erin leaving her like this, unfulfilled, was terrifying.

"Please, fuck me. I need you inside of me."

Erin's right thigh roughly pushed down between Alex's legs, parting them further. Alex felt pinned to the ground by Erin's weight on her and it was deliciously restricting.

She felt Erin's lips on her shoulder as Erin slid down her body a little. Suddenly, Erin's teeth dug into her shoulder and Alex felt a bite of possession and Erin sucked on her skin. Alex felt in the moment like she wanted Erin to devour her whole. Like Erin was a wolf on the mountain who had attacked her and was going to eat her, and it was the most wildly erotic thought Alex had ever had. She heard herself moaning wildly and panting, her breaths coming quickly, her desperation evident to her and obviously to Erin too.

She felt Erin's right hand pushing suddenly between her ass cheeks seeking access to her burning core. Erin's strong fingers probed roughly between Alex's legs. Alex felt so close to orgasm even at the thought of feeling Erin inside of her.

Alex had no desire to escape, but she liked the thought that she couldn't even if she wanted to. She was utterly pinned in place by Erin's bodyweight above her. She was entirely at Erin's mercy, pinned down for Erin to take in every way. Erin mouth was still sucking her shoulder. Alex knew there would be bruises there where Erin's mouth had been, and she liked thinking about them.

Alex felt Erin's fingers sliding through her wetness. They teased her for a further few seconds before they entered her deeply and firmly as though Alex's body was Erin's to take. Which it was, really, if Alex let herself think about it. Alex wanted to wrench her legs from her body to allow Erin better access to fuck her. As Erin's fingers pushed down on her G spot and began to fuck her firmly and deeply, Alex felt herself transporting to another world.

"Can I touch my clit?" she gasped breathily in between moans.

"Yes. Well done for asking. Good girl. I want you to ask permission before you come? Okay?"

"Okay," Alex murmured as she wriggled and managed to lift her hip enough to wedge her right hand underneath herself at her excited clitoris. Alex was too pressed down to be able to move her hand, but she found she could just hold it still and as

Erin's fingers fucked her she could grind her clit against her hand.

Erin's fingers hit their rhythm again and Alex teetered on the very edge. It felt like the most exquisite feeling in the world.

"Please. Please can I come?" she moaned.

"Yes. Come for me, Mrs. Kennedy," Erin whispered deeply in her ear, and Alex felt the whole world fall apart around her as Erin's words tipped her straight over the edge and into her orgasm. She felt lost in the rush of it through her body. Every part of her felt lost to it and lost to Erin. Her orgasm continued to throb through her as Erin's soft kisses peppered her neck and her shoulder and her ear. "You are so fucking beautiful, Mrs. Kennedy."

THEY MADE it home to the Scottish castle. The bedroom had a roaring log fire and it also had a huge copper bath at the end of the bed that the staff had run for them in preparation. The water was hot and had rose petals scattered in at Alex's request.

Getting warm and clean was an exquisite pleasure in this beautiful room. Alex felt feeling rush back to her body in the hot water. Erin looked beautiful with her hair wet and slicked back. There was a gentle peace to being in the bath together. Erin sat behind her and Alex fitted between her legs and leant back against her breasts and let Erin bathe her with a sponge and shower gel.

When they were done, they moved to relax and dry on towels and cushions in front of the open fire. Alex instinctively moved down Erin's body, settling between her legs, moving her mouth to return the pleasure that Erin had given her earlier. Erin had a slick wetness, even after the bath. Alex loved how her body told of her desire for her. Alex buried her tongue in Erin's wetness and watched as the golden light from the fire danced over her body as she relaxed and enjoyed it, her head propped up on cushions. Alex closed her eyes and relaxed into the task she adored and could do forever.

"Turn around." Alex looked up hearing Erin's command. "I want to taste

you while you fuck me," Erin said confidently.

Alex didn't need asking twice; she loved
to obey Erin. She spun around, lifting her
left leg to straddle Erin's face in a 69 position and she moved her own face back
down to bury it in the dark curls between
Erin's legs. Being shorter than Erin, it was
hard to reach with her mouth as Erin's
strong arms pulled Alex's hips back onto
her face. Alex moved her right hand between Erin's legs and pushed her fingers
inside her. She could reach with her fingers
at least, if not her mouth. She felt Erin sitting up further and raising her head to
push Alex forwards and allow Alex to reach
her with her mouth. Alex took Erin's clitoris in her mouth while she fucked her
slowly and deeply with her fingers. They
rocked together in a steady rhythm and
Alex felt Erin's tongue push inside her. She
could taste Erin's swollen clit in her mouth,
she could feel Erin's pussy tightening
around her fingers, she could feel Erin's orgasm building and as Erin's tongue pushed
deep inside her, Alex felt the magic of them
both orgasming at the same time in front of

the warmth of the fire. The orgasm felt warm, loving and like the most beautiful thing in the world.

She lay like that for a minute with her face against Erin's pubic hair, inhaling the scent of her, the magic of her. Feeling Erin's heart beating beneath her, feeling the warmth of Erin's smooth skin and the heat of Erin's breath on her inner thigh. Alex felt like they were the only people who existed in the whole world.

I love you so much.

5

E rin woke the next day to what felt like a magical new world, that of the Highlands of Scotland. Every day felt magical seeing Alex when she woke up. Princess Alexandra, naked and sleeping next to her, her face peaceful in sleep and her beauty more natural than it had ever been. They had breakfast delivered to their room and they followed it up with lazy sex in the big soft bed and clean sheets, gently devouring each other's bodies. Erin felt desire often when she woke up with Alex. Their chemistry was so strong, they rode a fine edge of electricity between them that threatened to descend into sex at any time. When they were alone together there was so much opportunity to feast on Alex's body and Erin did just that. She had woken up still tasting Alex's orgasm from the night before and she wanted more. Sometimes their sex was gentle and loving, sometimes passionate, raw and fierce, sometimes carefully controlled power games and role play. Erin loved every moment of it. She loved seeing Alex come apart in so many different ways. She loved having Alex pleasure her in so many different ways. Their sex that morning was lazy and sleepy. Erin wanted to taste Alex more and go down on her while she was half asleep. Alex's orgasm was long and slow but easily achieved, as was Erin's orgasm when Alex settled between her legs and made slow love to her with her mouth. Erin hadn't always found her own orgasm to be straightforward before her relationship with Alex. There had been times with previous partners where her orgasm had been temperamental or entirely elusive, but there was something about her connection with Alex that just let her relax and allow an orgasm to wash over her as Alex gave to her body.

They showered and dressed for the day and headed out to the grounds of the beautiful stone-built Scottish castle.

There was a collection of dogs that lived at the castle and Audrey had been delighted to meet them. They all wandered out with Erin and Alex on their little adventure.

Erin marvelled at the beauty of the countryside. She had never seen anything like these lochs and mountains and the wild openness that was northern Scotland. It was so freeing for Alex to just be anonymous because they were so isolated. They were out walking for hours and they didn't see a single other person other than the castle staff.

Erin loved how passionate Alex was about it. Alex wanted to teach her about the loch and the deer and the mountains. Alex loved this world and Erin was easily caught up in her love for it.

They swam nude again in the loch, this time in the morning sunshine, and the water definitely felt a few degrees warmer.

Erin was surprised that Alex was such a strong swimmer for someone so slight, but then she realised there was still probably a lot about Alex she didn't know and that she wanted to spend the rest of forever finding out.

Erin thought even though they were isolated it was risky for Alex to be nude in public in daylight. There was always the risk of a long lens on a paparazzi camera. But she didn't say anything. That was the security team's job, to form a distant protection around the loch when they were swimming.

Erin watched Alex as she emerged from the water, her skin and hair soaking wet and sleek like an otter. Her breasts were full and big on her small frame and her ribcage and hipbones were pronounced.

God, she is so beautiful in the sunlight.

Erin worried for a second about the possibility of the security team watching her from a distance with binoculars and then she thought Alex had probably considered that and got off on it, this tiny sliver of simple freedom she was indulging in,

being nude in the open and the slight potential of being watched.

Erin watched the lovely lines and the
way the light fell on her wet skin as she
raised her hands to dry her hair with a
towel. They had come better prepared than
they had last night. Erin dried herself with
a towel and Alex leaned into her and kissed
her. There was something so simple and
beautiful and free about kissing naked in
the sunlight. Feeling Alex's wet, cool skin
press against her own, her nipples prom-
inent and bullet-like from the cold water
felt arousing.

Erin knew that unfortunately they
couldn't fuck on the heather in the daylight
in front of a potential audience, however
much she wanted to.

Erin had done a lot of swimming as a
child, although most of it had been in
pools, occasionally in the sea on a family
holiday. She had never ventured into this
wild swimming in lakes and rivers, and it
felt utterly refreshing and amazing. So
much in the UK, people worried about the
safety of things like this. People in the
modern world had forgotten how to truly

live. How to feel the sun on their skin and the wind in their hair. They had forgotten how to enjoy themselves like children, and Erin was so grateful to Alex for introducing her to the loch swimming and the freedom of the wide expanse of water all to themselves.

"Can we bring a ball down here to play tomorrow? Do you have anything like that at the castle?"

"Ah, we should, for sure. If not, I'll send someone out for one. Like a bouncy beach volleyball or water polo ball-type thing?"

"Yeah, if we go in to a depth where we can still touch the floor we can play with the ball."

Alex smiled in the sunshine, now safely wrapped up in a big towel that drowned her. There was a lightness to Alex on this holiday that Erin hadn't seen before. It was as though Alex had left all her duty and the weight of her responsibility in London and underneath all that was a layer of sweet-ness and childlike fun that Erin adored. Alex reached for her hand, weaving her small cold fingers into Erin's and then nuz-zling herself in under Erin's arm.

"Right, we should get dressed and head back. Nicolas should be arriving at some point. Also, I'm starving!"

"Me too. What are we having for lunch?"

"I requested macaroni pies followed by deep fried Mars bars. Scottish traditions." Alex's eyes glinted naughtily.

"No way! I mean I had heard the Scottish would put anything in a pie, but macaroni?"

"Don't knock it. It is a revelation. And you just wait till a deep fried Mars bar goes in your mouth. A taste sensation!"

"I guess we will be drinking Irn-Bru too?" Erin asked. She actually loved the famous Scottish soda.

"Of course. Irn-Bru is compulsory!" Alex laughed as she pulled her dress over her head.

Erin pulled on her shorts and her sports bra. It was so hot, she hadn't bothered with a T-shirt.

She scooped Alex up in her arms and Alex squealed.

"This macaroni pie had better be good, Mrs. Kennedy, or I'll have to eat you in-

stead!" Alex laughed and wriggled in a
halfhearted attempt to escape. Erin held
her tight and kissed her and felt Alex melt
in her arms.

BACK AT THE CASTLE, Prince Nicolas had arrived and joined them for lunch.

"So, I have just been to the Edinburgh
Fertility Clinic." He smiled. "There is no
pressure of any kind, but I just want you
both to know if you did want to use me as a
donor, I have left a donation and it's in a
freezer in the clinic. They checked it out
under the microscope and it all looks good
to go. I wouldn't ever be offended if you decide against it. I know this is such a huge
decision for you both and I'm happy to be
able to help if it is something you want."

Erin smiled. "Wow, thanks, Nicolas, you
didn't hang around!"

"No point really. Whether you use it or
not is up to you two. But I'm happy to offer,
so it may as well be there ready in case you
want it."

"We have talked about this so much and

we really *really* appreciate your offer. How do you feel about it?" Erin asked him. Nicolas looked awkward and bashful as he answered. His blonde hair was longer and falling across his face.

"I, um, I love the idea. I know I wouldn't be a father, I would be a donor, and I would never ever overstep that. I just, I always wanted children and this is a way of doing it. I mean, I don't know how you would feel, but I would like to have some contact with the child, just to be able to see them, and see how they are doing and if there is ever anything you needed, I would be there. But...only if that was okay?"

"Oh, Nicolas. Erin and I have spoken at length about it. We both find you absolutely the most respectful guy, and as long as you respect that Erin and I will be the child's parents and we will be on the birth certificate, we want you to take a role in the child's life. We would ideally like to publicly announce you as the donor and to allow you to have an 'uncle' type role in the child's life. We would like them to know about their Swedish heritage as well as their British side. If you wanted, they could

be Prince or Princess of Sweden as well as
of Great Britain."

Nicolas's face lit up. "Really? Oh, I
would adore that. Would that be okay? Se-
riously? Erin, how would you feel about
that?"

Erin smiled. She was happy he was
happy. She absolutely agreed with Alex
that they wanted the child to know about
his or her history and to have an opportunity to have a relationship with Nicolas.
"I'm absolutely in agreement with Alex
here. We want you to be a part of our child's
life. We cannot think of a better role model
for our child to have in their life. If you are
okay with it. I think officially Alex needs to
get Julia to put it all in writing in a contract
for you to sign, but we absolutely want you
to be a part of it all if you want to."

Nicolas's smile was wide. He had a
lovely, kind face and Erin noticed that his
eyes were dark green perhaps similar to her
own. Erin had thought at length about
what was important to her in a donor and it
went far beyond physical qualities. She felt
strongly that a child couldn't have too
much love, and having someone as loyal

and noble as Nicolas in the child's life could be no bad thing.

"I'm in. I can't think of anything I would love more. Well, as soon as you want it, if you still want it, I'm happy to sign anything and you can go to the clinic and get the rest of it done yourself."

Erin felt Alex's hand seek out her own and squeeze it under the table.

Erin smiled and took a big mouthful of the macaroni pie. The dense cheesiness of the pasta was delicious inside the pie crust. This was Scottish junk food at its finest.

"You were right about this macaroni pie, Mrs. Kennedy."

Alex laughed. Nicolas looked confused. "I have honestly never tasted anything like it in my life." Erin laughed too. "You wait till you try the dessert."

Maybe this was the beginning of her family. Erin had always known her family wouldn't have a traditional look to it. This was the beginning of it. Their child would be a mix of Nicolas, Alex and herself even though its genetics would only match that of Nicolas and Alex, it still felt kind of magical. Erin imagined what he or she might look like and might be like. She imagined a tiny Alex going around everywhere with them, and she liked the idea of it. Erin wasn't close to her own family, but she suddenly felt a real drive to create a family to be close to.

This was the beginning of her family and she liked it.

LATER THAT DAY, Vic bowled into the castle like a whirlwind. Erin found her on the floor in the grand hallway making friends with all the dogs who all immediately adored her. She was covered in dog hair and slobber.

"Victoria. You made it." Erin smiled. "I would hug you, but I don't fancy the dog hair."

Vic laughed loudly. "Fucking precious are we now you are some kind of Princess, Bodyguard? Guess what, I bought three fucking horses."

"Wow. Where on earth did you find the money for them?"

"Sold Romeo for a small fortune last

week. The Romeo money will keep me going for a while. Bought these three cheap young horses, I'll train them up, keep them a while then hopefully sell them for a small fortune too."

"Ah, I loved Romeo," Erin said fondly. "Will you miss him?"

"Oh, for sure," said Vic. "But that's my horsey life. I buy, I train, I sell. Repeat. I love seeing them progress after they move on from me. I love thinking I took that horse when it was young and dumb and gave it the basics, gave it the best start in life for a brilliant future. Then some idiot with too much money like you and the Princess buys them from me and I start again with a new one."

"What do these three look like?"

"Oh, there is a stunning black horse. Difficult and problematic but hellishly talented. If I can tame him and get him to trust, he will jump the moon. I have high hopes."

"What are you going to call him?"

"Well, they are calling him Satan," Vic roared with laughter. "So maybe I will keep that. He broke the fucking stable girl's leg last week." She literally rolled on the floor laughing with the dogs rolling around with her and jumping on her. Erin wasn't so sure that a horse called Satan who broke the legs of stable girls was something to laugh about, but that was Vic all over, completely unfazed by so-called dangerous horses.

"They are going to deliver them down south next week. I'm going to call the other two Angel and God to fit the theme."

Vic laughed more and the assortment of dogs loved it.

Erin laughed. She could never quite understand what on earth went on in Vic's crazy mind, but there she was, happy with the dogs and the purchase of her new horses, Satan, Angel and God.

That evening they headed into Edinburgh in disguise. Alex wore the same long dark wig that she had worn for that secret night in Soho, the first time they had kissed. It never failed to amaze Erin how different someone as instantly recognisable as Princess Alexandra could look when she had an entirely different hairstyle, coloured contact lenses and dressed like a teenage lesbian in ripped jeans with heavy black eye makeup. She looked not a day over eighteen years old, and Erin barely recognised her. The difficulty this time was that Erin was now also hugely recognisable so needed to be disguised too.

Erin was sitting at the dressing table and Alex looked her up and down with a thoughtful look on her face. (Even if her face looked nothing like her actual face.) "So, I can dress you *however* I want?" Alex pouted.

Erin laughed. "Why do I feel like I am going to totally regret this?"

"Well, I am going to have *so* much fun at least." Alex smiled widely. "Right, let's start with your face, then we can try some wigs on.

Erin always enjoyed Alex doing her makeup. Alicia definitely created a more natural look when she was in charge of Erin's makeup, but there was something very intimate about Alex touching her face and looking intently at her as she concentrated on what she was doing. Erin was very unsure about the false eyelashes, but they went on, and she was handed light blue contact lenses, which she struggled to get in. She turned to look at herself in the mirror and gasped.

"Well, I barely recognise myself, so I think you have done a good job!"

Alex smiled with pride. "I'm not done yet, let's get one of these wigs on you."

Erin was relieved to see Alex pick up a dark-coloured wig. She thought blonde would be one step too far on her.

Alex positioned it on her head, her own hair was already slicked back so was hidden immediately. The wig was long, dark brown curls and it had the desired effect of absolutely hiding her identity.

The door banged and Vic strode in followed by three dogs. Audrey was not amongst them. Since she had found her little dog gang in her Scottish paradise, Audrey had been quite happy doing her own thing with them. Erin always thought Vic was like the Pied Piper for dogs. They always just adored her and would follow her anywhere. For someone who didn't have her own dog, she always seemed to have the nearest dog looking at her with eternal loyalty.

"Fuck me, you look hot, Bodyguard. Entirely didn't recognise you. And Princess, you look about fourteen years old."

Alex laughed. "Good job I have a fake passport then, isn't it? There are definitely perks to Princess life. They had the actual passport office whip up a fake for me. It wouldn't get me on an airplane, but it will certainly get me into an Edinburgh bar."

"Well, I have news. We aren't going to a bar. Well, I mean we may well end up in a bar, but first and foremost, we are going on a ghost tour."

There was a moment of silence from both Erin and Alex.

"I told Nicolas and he was fucking *delighted.* Edinburgh is *so* old and *so* obviously haunted that I can't think of a better plan for the evening. There are underground vaults on this tour where like a million people died and everything."

Erin laughed.

"Only you, Vic, only you."

"Bars are boring. Ghost tours are where it is at. Fact."

"I think I am overdressed for a ghost tour. Can I lose the fake eyelashes?"

"Absolutely not," Alex responded. "You are a total femme for one night only. Although, given that we are going to be walking round the city I will let you off wearing a dress. You can wear ripped jeans and converse like me if you like."

"Thank fuck for that!" Erin and Vic both said at the same time. Alex laughed.

"Well, it is a well-known fact that girls who walk with swag like Erin does should not wear dresses. It never works!"

"Now I know why I don't wear dresses," Erin said drily.

THE GHOST TOUR was actually fun and interesting. Their tour guide wore a long, black cloak with a hood and told them creepy stories from times past, and they walked through the Edinburgh Old Town learning things about the city that Erin would never have learnt otherwise. The buildings were tall and the streets were narrow, stemming from a time when they were built to cram in as many occupants as possible. There was a light fog over the city lending an extra creepy air to the tour. Edinburgh was a couple of hours drive south from where the castle was in the Highlands, so there was darkness in Edinburgh. Darkness and this light fog fell over them as they wandered down the damp walled alleyways that were shrouded in a strange silence.

It made a stark contrast to the bustling Edinburgh tourist zone of the Royal Mile where Erin had visited before. She could only imagine the contrast to the Palace at Holyrood that was owned by Alex's family. Holyrood Palace was the King's Edinburgh residence and the epitome of luxury and it was amazed Erin that it was really was only a stone's throw away from the creepy streets they now walked behind their cloaked tour guide.

They finally made it to the underground vaults underneath the city streets. There was a damp mustiness to them and they were pitch black. Their journey was marked by candlelight. The tour guide told stories of years ago when these tiny, strange caves were inhabited by the poorest people in Edinburgh. Twenty or thirty people crammed into one of these vaults that now struggled to hold the ten of them that were on the tour. Erin couldn't even stand up properly for fear of banging her head on the ceiling. These people lived here in poverty so many years ago with no sanitation and no running water. So many of them died in these horrific conditions with no daylight and their spirits are said to haunt the vaults.

Erin didn't believe in spirits, but this place did feel creepy and sad. So very sad. She couldn't imagine the people that had died crammed into these tiny airless spaces. She wondered how it would hit Alex, how she felt about poverty. Although it was from such a long time ago, Erin deeply felt it and looking at Alex's over made-up face in the candlelight, she could see that Alex did too. Maybe there was something they could do in the future, to help people living in poverty across the world.

Erin was relieved when they made it out of the vaults and back above ground and she gulped in the fresh air in the welcome open darkness of the city.

They went to a couple of bars for drinks and successfully nobody recognised them, which Alex revelled in.

The Range Rovers collected them for the long car journey back to the castle where it still wasn't dark, and Erin was happy to lose the wig and wash off the makeup and snuggle into bed with Alex. Real Alex, blonde Alex—Alex as she was supposed to be.

Erin felt the great privilege that they had and she wanted to use it to do more good in the world.

6

A few days later, Nicolas had left to head back to Sweden having signed the papers that Alex had Julia send up from London. Alex sat looking at the signed papers in the morning when she suddenly looked up at Erin. "Shall we just do it? When I'm ovulating next? Shall we just try the insemination at the clinic and see what happens?"

Erin smiled back at her reassuringly. "Let's try. Let's make a little family." Erin leant over and kissed her deeply, and the scariest thing in Alex's world suddenly felt less scary with Erin by her side.

DR. ANNA KELLER had been flown into Edinburgh at Alex's request, and Alex and Erin had moved into Holyrood Palace in Edinburgh for a week to complete some public appearances and to be close to the fertility clinic so they could do the insemination on the right day for Alex's cycle.

Alex had been going in for a couple of days to get a scan which would tell Dr. Keller the right time to do the insemination.

As Alex laid back for yet another scan and felt the probe and the lube cold inside of her, Erin sat by her holding her hand and watching the monitor. Dr. Keller always talked them through what she could see. This time all she said was, "It is time. Do you want to go for it?"

Alex felt overwhelmed for a second. She had always known she would do this but the actual act of trying to become pregnant suddenly felt too huge to comprehend.

Erin squeezed her hand and nodded encouragingly but deferring to Alex as she always had. "I will support you with whatever you decide, but it is your body and it is absolutely your choice."

Alex looked to Dr. Keller and nodded. "Yes, let's do it. Will it hurt?"

"You might feel a little pain as we go through the cervix, but it won't last. I'll be as quick as I can."

Alex watched as Dr. Keller and her assistant prepared the equipment and the semen for the IUI. "This is so weird," Alex couldn't help commenting.

"Do you wish we were doing it at home? Because it isn't too late? We can do that, right, Dr. Keller?" Erin looked concerned.

"No, honestly, I am fine. Let's just get it done. Dr. Keller has been up there enough times now that the romance is certainly dead."

Dr. Keller laughed loudly and Alex admired her striking looks and bold red lipstick. Anna Keller always looked immaculate.

"Okay, I'm ready. Try and relax." Dr. Keller positioned herself between Alex's legs.

Alex tipped her head back so she wasn't

watching and closed her eyes. Erin squeezed her hand. There was a brief second of pain and then the pain stopped and there was a slightly uncomfortable feeling. Alex focussed on breathing deeply.

"Okay, I'm done." Dr. Keller leaned back and withdrew her equipment.

"Really?" Alex sat up and opened her eyes. "That's it?"

"That's it." Dr. Keller smiled at her. "Now we wait. We book you in for a pregnancy test in 14 days."

Alex smiled. It was so much easier than she had anticipated. She looked up at Erin. "Now we wait," she smiled.

THE DAYS FOLLOWING the insemination felt strange to Alex. Her body felt no different but she was constantly trying to feel something. She was hoping to feel changes as though she might feel an egg implanting and beginning to develop. She took things easy as advised. They stayed in Edinburgh a couple more days and she appeared publicly with Erin posing for photos, meeting people, signing autographs. All she could think of in the back of her mind was what might be happening inside of her body.

When they made it back to the castle in the Highlands, she waited a few days doing very little apart from walking around the estate with the dogs. Then on Dr. Keller's advice she recommenced the Loch swimming and some steady horse riding around the beautiful highlands with Erin.

Vic was around and highly supportive. She kept offering to put her ear to Alex's belly and declaring that she would be able to tell if she was pregnant. Alex allowed her to and laughed as Vic pushed up her shirt and laid her head against Alex's skin, listening intently and then declaring loudly that there was a baby in there.

On the fourteenth day they headed back to the clinic to be met by Dr. Keller who welcomed them with open arms. She embraced Alex and kissed her on her cheek. "Right, we will do a blood test. It will give us the most accurate answer."

Alex watched as the needle entered a vein on the inside of her elbow. Dr. Keller's practiced hands were confident as they inserted it. Alex watched her blood flow into the small vial. What would the answer be?

Dr. Keller withdrew the needle and pressed a piece of cotton wool to the wound in Alex's arm.

"Okay, give me a minute." Dr. Keller left the room.

"Oh god, I really hope this is it," Alex said. "I know people have to go through it multiple times sometimes to get a positive test and I will if I have to, but I just really hope it worked this time. I hate how invasive this all is. Dr. Keller is great, but I just wish it could just be us, you know. I think straight people just don't realise how easy they have it."

Erin kissed her forehead, and Alex felt the familiar love that always came from Erin's kisses alongside the electric rush that came from the touch of Erin's lips. "However long it takes, we will do it. For sure." Erin smiled as the door opened and Dr. Keller came back in.

"Well, no need to keep repeating IUI, we got you, first time. You are pregnant, Alexandra. Congratulations!"

Alex jumped up from the chair she realised she was still seated in. It felt surreal, like it was happening to someone else. Erin lifted her up in her strong arms and swung her round. Alex felt like she was dreaming when Erin kissed her.

"This is the beginning of everything, Lex. We have it all to come. I can't wait to have a family with you."

7

A couple of weeks later, Erin still couldn't believe it. It seemed quite unbelievable and Alex's body hadn't changed, but inside it must be changing. She felt so tender towards Alex, as though Alex needed extra care, and while physically this wasn't true, Erin could see the toll it was taking on Alex mentally. While Erin knew that Alex had always resigned herself to her duty of having children to have heirs to the throne, she also knew that Alex wasn't sure herself if it was something she would have done otherwise. Alex had only dared say it to her late at night in the safety of darkness when they were in bed together that she wasn't sure she wanted to be pregnant and to give birth. That in another world, if she wasn't Princess Alexandra and the rules on biological Royal heirs didn't exist, then maybe she would have liked to adopt or something. The thought of being pregnant seemed scary and overwhelming to her, even though she had spent a lifetime preparing for it.

It was one thing to consider the idea of *trying* to create a child. It was another thing entirely to experience the reality of pregnancy, the reality of it actually happening, that a child was in fact growing inside Alex every second of every day at the moment. Waiting for the first scan seemed like such a long wait. Erin wanted to know that everything looked normal and everything would be okay. Alex seemed fragile and Erin wasn't sure she would cope well if things went wrong with this pregnancy.

The only people they had told were Vic and Nicolas and Julia and all were delighted. Vic was like a child running round screaming and then when the staff looked surprised, she had to pretend she was excited about something else.

Erin would like to have thought they could trust the staff, but they kept the secrets from them the same as they did anyone else. All it would take would be one of them to sell to a journalist that Alex was pregnant and it would be in every newspaper in the world. They needed time to adjust to it themselves before the whole world found out. So they continued their normal activities, the swimming and the horse riding, and they stayed in Scotland. It seemed safer up there, so much more isolated, away from the real world and the news and being such a famous couple.

Alex and Erin were taking lunch in the gardens when Vic returned from a morning out fishing with one of the estate workers.

She plonked herself down at the table and helped herself to a chunk of bread from the table smearing a great chunk of butter onto it with a knife and biting into it.

"Ugh. That's better. I'm so fucking hungry."

Vic took another big bite. Her hands looked filthy.

"Right. I need to tell you both some-thing. Kind of a big thing. I've been kind of keeping it to myself a few days because well, you'll see. So sorry if I have been acting weird."

"Vic, you are always weird," Alex said.

"That's as may be, but this will be a shock to everyone. I think I'm pregnant."

"What?" Erin coughed. Alex's eyes were wide with shock. "Are you joking?" she asked.

"I *wish* I was. So I was feeling a bit weird and I missed my period so I figured I'll just take a test to be sure. And, well. It was posi-tive. So I went back to the chemist in that small town and bought 10 more tests—I swear they thought I was mad. Anyway, they were all positive."

Alex looked at her curiously. "Um, con-gratulations? Sorry if I am missing some-thing here, but how did this happen?"

"Your title ceremony with the King. There was that party in the palace after-wards. Two glasses of wine. Duke of Leices-ter. One-night stand on the big balcony at the palace. Sex was pretty good, but I've had better. He is a bit annoying, but I had

had wine and didn't care. I was on the pill, but if I'm honest with myself I'm not the best at remembering to take it. So, here we are."

"Jesus," Alex said.

"Are you going to tell him?" Erin asked.

"Fuck, no. I mean, I don't know what to do. I keep thinking I should get an abortion, then I look at the effort you two have had to put in to get pregnant, then I think abortions are bad and I should just go with what nature intended or something. Fuck. I don't know. I don't really think abortions are bad. I just, well it's just a little out of left field."

"I mean, you could just go for it? Then our kids can grow up together. You aren't in a bad position for being a single mum. We would help you. We have staff who would help."

"Fuck, Princess. Thanks, but it just all seems too much to comprehend right now, if you get me?"

"Okay, well, if nothing else, I'm going to have you booked in with Dr. Keller. You need to know for sure and you need to know what your options are, and she is exactly the woman to help you with that."

"Thank you." Vic seemed young suddenly.

"Duke of Leicester, though?" Alex screwed up her face. "He is *so* annoying!"

"Tell me about it!" Vic laughed.

ERIN AND ALEX decided to stay in Scotland till after their first scan and then head home afterwards. There were things that Alex needed to sort out, the King would need to be informed, and Alex and Erin needed to meet with Julia and figure out a plan going forwards, a plan for when to tell the press, a plan for the birth, a plan for the first weeks with the baby. There was so much more to having a baby in the public eye than Erin had ever thought of.

Vic had attended her appointment with Dr. Keller and her pregnancy had been confirmed and her options had been presented to her. Erin knew that Vic felt grateful that she lived in a country where abortion was an option, but Vic hadn't made a decision yet. She didn't know what to do. She had confided in Erin that it only made it harder to make a decision when Alex was pregnant with a pregnancy that had been so carefully planned and created, whereas Vic had exactly the opposite—a pregnancy resulting from ten minutes of a casual fuck with someone she didn't want to pursue a relationship with.

The weight of the pending decision or perhaps of the pregnancy itself was weighing on Vic's shoulders. Erin saw it in her, she seemed to flick between childlike and vulnerable and suddenly grown up, pondering her options and the consequences of each and every one. Erin was there to talk to her when she wanted to talk, but ultimately the decision was one she had to make herself.

Erin saw in Alex confusion over how she felt about Vic's pregnancy and perhaps her own too. Alex had suffered a little with nausea and sickness but nothing too bad. Vic's had been worse.

Alex wasn't talking much about the baby, she seemed to be waiting, just to see if it was all real, just to see if anything went wrong before she committed to the idea that she would soon become a mother.

THEY ARRIVED at the Edinburgh clinic and were ushered straight through to Dr. Keller, who was immaculate in a sky blue pantsuit and navy blue heels.

"Lovely to see you, Alexandra, Erin. A pleasure as always. Right, let's get you on this table and let's have a first look at this little one." Dr. Keller wasted no time.

Alex was keen to know so she was quick in getting herself sorted and getting on the table. Dr. Keller moved between Alex's legs and inserted the ultrasound probe in place.

Alex and Erin watched keenly on the monitor as Dr. Keller began to move the probe and describe what she was seeing in images.

Suddenly, Dr. Keller looked surprised. "Aha," she said.

"What, what is it?" Alex looked immediately concerned.

Dr. Keller studied the monitor more closely. "So, we have an embryo here." She pointed with her free hand to the monitor. "Then," she moved the probe slightly and continued, "It is early days, but I am pretty confident we have another embryo just here." She pointed to the monitor again. "I can't be one hundred percent at the moment, but I think you are expecting twins.

Alex looked at Erin anxiously for reassurance.

"That's great news. Isn't it?" Erin felt an ominous air had descended on the room. Alex looked anxious and Dr. Keller looked serious.

"Well, it is if all goes well. It does increase the risk of miscarriage and it does make Alex's pregnancy high risk. I want to monitor you carefully throughout, Alex. We need to give it a couple of weeks before we take another look on a scan and hopefully, we will have more answers then. It really is too early to see a lot at the moment. We will reconvene in London and I will have more answers for you."

8

Alex had a helicopter organised to fly them home from Scotland. She loved trips in the helicopter and she hadn't wanted to sit in the Range Rover for ten hours. She felt lost in thought about the potential babies. Twins wasn't something she had considered. Twins were also a little more complex when it came to the line of succession to the throne. Well, not entirely, whichever twin came out first was deemed older and therefore the heir to the throne. They had done everything they could to ensure their children would be legitimate heirs to the throne. There were those that would argue that since Erin wasn't their biological father, that even though she and Erin were married, the children would not be legitimate, but the King had amended the ruling to include children born to a same-sex marriage. He was determined to support Alex and for that she would be eternally grateful. Twins, though. What did it mean? What did Dr. Keller's face mean? Alex had researched the risks of twin pregnancy. Higher risk of miscarriage. Higher risk of premature birth. Higher risk of a number of pregnancy complications that Alex had never heard of. God, she felt so unprepared for this. She had been anxious about pregnancy anyway and here she was typically getting a complicated one.

She had spoken to Erin at great length about it. Erin had her imagining the two little babies being born, everything working out perfectly, and Alex wanted so badly to believe that but she had this feeling inside her that everything might not be okay.

She was happy to be home but she couldn't face public engagements so she had Jess tell her PR manager that she was unwell and would be taking some time to recuperate and everything was to be put on hold until she felt better.

Erin was happy to be home and she spent her mornings at the stables with Shimmer and Vic and her afternoons being extra caring to Alex.

ALEX FELT her body begin to change slightly. She felt her breasts becoming heavier and more tender. If she looked carefully, she could notice a slight swelling in her abdomen. It was so minor that she knew nobody else would notice, perhaps not even Erin. But Erin had noticed her breasts, it was hard not to. Alex passed the time till the next scan. She needed to see Dr. Keller. She needed to know more.

WHEN THE DAY finally came for the next scan, Alex felt irrationally terrified.

"It'll be okay, you know, Lex. You and your babies will have the best of everything. Dr. Keller is the best in her field. Nothing bad is going to happen. Even if it is twins, we will be alright. You've only got six more months to go of pregnancy. I'm right here for you, for everything."

Alex clutched Erin's hand as they headed into the London clinic and straight through to Dr. Keller's consult room.

"Morning, Alexandra, morning, Erin. Let's get a good look what is going on today. I will be able to see a lot more. We can make a plan."

When the probe entered Alex cold with lube, she winced. It felt invasive today, as though she didn't want it inside of her. She had counted the days until this scan and yet she didn't want it. She had a bad feeling.

Dr. Keller was moving the probe and studying the monitor but she wasn't saying anything.

Alex lay back and closed her eyes.

"What's happening, Doctor?" asked Erin. "What do you see?"

"Is it bad?" Alex mumbled. "What's wrong with them?"

Dr. Keller took another minute to study various angles before answering.

"Alexandra. Open your eyes. I don't want you to panic, but I need to talk to both of you. There are three babies. Triplets. As I am sure you have read up on the risks of twin pregnancies, the risks just multiply as we move to triplet pregnancies. Now, each fetus, as far as I can tell, looks alright so far. One looks a little small." She sighed and sat back in her chair. "I'm going to need to be totally honest with you here even though it might sound brutal. You should know we are 100% looking at a high-risk pregnancy here. There is a risk of losing all of them. There is a significant risk of premature birth. There are much higher risks of birth and developmental defects. I need you to think about your options."

"What? What options?" Erin said. Alex felt numb.

"Selective reduction is an option," Dr. Keller said calmly.

"What? Like an abortion of one of them?" Erin asked.

"Or two," Dr. Keller replied. "Given who Alexandra is and who the potential future child will be, I have to recommend selective reduction."

Alex felt tears starting to fall from her eyes. "I knew something bad was coming," she sobbed. Alex looked at Erin, who was crying too. Strong reliable Erin was crying. Alex thought how rarely she had seen Erin cry. Erin hugged her and kissed her face, kissing each tear away while Dr. Keller put her equipment away quietly and lifted Alex's legs gently down from the stirrups pulling her dress down for her.

"It is a simple procedure. I can give you a week to make the decision, ideally. It will give you the best chance of a healthy child, a healthy heir to the throne. Okay, I know you need time to take in this information. I'm going to put it all in email for you so you can read and digest all of the risks, so you know exactly what we are looking at here."

Erin nodded as Alex numbly went about putting her underwear and shoes back on. She felt like the world was crumbling around her, inside of her. The only people who knew or were allowed to know were her and Erin and Dr. Keller.

The journey home was in silence with

Erin holding her hand tightly. Neither of them had any words yet.

A 12-week scan was supposed to be the time you announced your pregnancy to others. Alex had the whole world to announce her pregnancy to, yet what was she supposed to say?

If she aborted two of the babies, did she keep that secret and just announce her pregnancy of one to the world? What if people found out? She would be a monster that killed babies. Could she kill two of her babies, or even one? Selective reduction. What a stupid term. It was abortion whatever name you tried to give it. Not that Alex was against abortion; she was such a big believer in a woman's right to choose and she knew she would completely support Vic if she decided to abort. But not for herself. Not now.

Alex suddenly realised how fiercely she wanted these babies, that despite her anxieties and her misgivings, she wanted them so badly. All three of them.

In bed that night, Erin held her while she cried. She pressed her face to Erin's breast and cried and cried with her anxieties from the past few weeks spilling out in her tears.

THE FOLLOWING DAY, they sat with Vic and explained to her what was happening.

"Fuck, guys, I'm so sorry."

"Have you made a decision about what you are going to do yet?" Alex looked to Vic.

"Um, yes. I've booked in for a termination with Dr. Keller for tomorrow."

Alex looked at her. Her oldest friend. One of her only close friends. She was having an abortion.

"God, I'm sorry. I guess I just thought you would keep it. I'm sorry I haven't been there for you enough lately. I just—"

"Princess, you don't need to explain. You have plenty of your own shit to worry about. Plus, me being pregnant and/or having an abortion is complex for you right now. Even more so since this recent news."

"How did you decide in the end?"

"I wouldn't be a good mother. I just

don't think I'm maternal enough. I'm terrified I would fuck it up."

"You wouldn't, you know. If you just need someone to tell you that, then I can tell you that. I think you would make a great mum. See how all those dogs adore you. Your kid would adore you just the same."

Tears ran down Vic's cheeks. "I'm sorry," Alex said. "I shouldn't have said that when you already made your decision."

Vic wiped her eyes on her sleeve and looked up. "Fuck, sorry. No time for being dramatic here. What will you two do?"

"I know what all the science says and usually I'm quite a rational person. I know it is most likely the best thing to do for a positive outcome. I also know because of who I am, there is so much more pressure to have a live and healthy birth."

"But you don't want to do it?" Vic read between the lines. Alex shook her head. "It's funny, I wasn't sure to start with about pregnancy. I was never sure I wanted kids; I was doing it just because. The start of my pregnancy I never felt like a mother-earth type, yet now two of my babies are threatened and I feel fiercely—and probably naively—protective. I want them all to have a chance."

"How about you, Bodyguard?"

"God, I don't want to do it either. But Dr. Keller was so sure it is the right thing. I worry about Alex too. It isn't just the babies at risk, it's her too."

"And she is Princess Fucking Alexandra. So I guess poor old Dr. Keller has a lot of pressure on her to prioritise the survival of her most VIP client. It won't look good for her if she kills you off, Princess."

Alex felt torn between her duty to her country and her duty to her unborn children.

"Can we all look at the evidence she sent through on email together and try and look at it objectively? Vic, are you in?"

Vic took a deep breath. "I'm in."

"Right." Erin brought the email up on her iPad and started reading aloud.

Alex focussed and tried to think what she would advise someone else to do in her position. There wasn't an obvious answer. With triplets, sure it was high-risk and potentially complicated, but it wouldn't be insanity to continue the pregnancy with all of them. But could she forgive herself if they all ended up dying?

"Do you think we should discuss it with Julia or your father?" Erin asked.

"I don't need any more pressure or more people knowing. This has to be between the three of us and Dr. Keller until we decide what to do."

"Okay." Erin nodded compliance and so did Vic.

Alex felt something inside her. She figured it was unlikely to be pregnancy related and she was probably imagining it, but it was still there. She knew in that moment that she couldn't end these babies. Any of them.

She took a deep breath. "Okay, I need to keep them all. I need to give them all a chance. I cannot contemplate any other option. Erin, are you with me?"

Erin smiled at her. "Of course, you know I am. We will do everything right. We will give it every chance. Let's see Dr. Keller tomorrow and make a plan."

Alex felt better for the decision being made. She knew they would do everything to give these babies a chance at life. "Even if they have health problems or developmental problems, whatever it is, we can handle it. If anyone can, we can."

Erin smiled and kissed her. "We absolutely can."

Alex felt terrible when she looked at Vic. She knew Vic was also seeing Dr. Keller the following day for entirely different reasons. Vic smiled weakly and left the room.

9

"We want to keep them all. We will do whatever it takes. We want to give them all every chance. Can you support us in that?" Alex said boldly as she gripped Erin's hand tightly.

Dr. Keller smiled and sat down opposite them. "I thought you might say that. In that case, congratulations! I will support you in every way to give these babies every chance. It is still possible that one or more may struggle to thrive in pregnancy, in which case we still may need to reconsider losing one or more to save the other at a later stage."

"Thank you." Alex looked relieved. "Absolutely, I understand that. But if they look alright, let's keep giving all three every chance."

"Alexandra, Erin, I am 100 percent on your side. I will do everything I can for you both and the babies. You have my word. I'll monitor you carefully though the next few months, but we need to be prepared that best-case scenario with no major complications we are probably looking at early labour at about 32 weeks—that is eight weeks earlier than a normal pregnancy. I think a scheduled C-section would be the safest option. If they are born at this stage, they are likely to need a stay in the Neonatal Intensive Care Unit. We will know a lot more as we go. But this is the best-case scenario that they are all born at a reasonable time and in reasonable health."

Alex and Erin nodded eagerly.

"Okay, wonderful." Dr. Keller folded her notebook and stood up.

"You are seeing our friend, Victoria Grey-Hughes this afternoon, right?" Erin asked.

"I am," Dr. Keller sighed.

"Look after her," Erin said as she helped Alex up. She knew Alex didn't need help. Not yet, but she probably would as things progressed. Erin could see the beginnings of swelling in her belly and she could only imagine what Alex would look like as three babies grew in Alex's tiny body.

She knew Alex was worried about Vic. They had both offered to go with her to her appointment, but she had said she would rather go alone.

Erin really hoped she would be okay.

BACK AT THE CASTLE, Vic picked up the phone and called through to Julia Wilding, Alex's personal advisor. Vic knew that Julia was in the castle for a meeting with Alex later. Julia would just be working away in her office space until Alex was ready for her.

Vic didn't know why she did it as she sat on her bed contemplating life and her afternoon plans with Dr. Keller, but she sat holding the phone.

"Julia Wilding," Julia answered the

phone brightly and efficiently. Her voice was as smooth as silk.

"Um, Julia, hi, it's Victoria." Vic felt stupid. What the fuck was she doing?

"Victoria?" Julia enquired.

Fuck, she doesn't even know who I am.

"Victoria Grey-Hughes. Alex's friend."

"Oh, Victoria. Of course. What can I do for you? Is everything okay?"

"Fuck, sorry, I shouldn't have called you. Of course, everything is fine. It doesn't matter. I'm sorry to have bothered you." Vic was about to hang up.

Julia's voice was kind and filled with empathy. "If there's something, anything I can help with, please, just ask. I have time. Are you in the castle? I'll come to you."

"Um, I'm in my room. If you turn right at the top of the stairs on the third floor, I'm the third door on the right."

What the fuck am I doing? Princess will be mad.

Vic had spent so long avoiding all the important people despite living in the castle. She wanted an easy life and that didn't involve being around the important people and having to be on her best behaviour.

She had lied to Erin and Alex when they asked if she wanted them to go with her to her appointment and said she would rather go alone.

She wouldn't rather go alone. She suddenly felt lonelier than she ever had and she actually often felt lonely despite her self proclaimed 'Lone Wolf' status. She was eternally grateful to Alex and Erin for taking her in. They *got* her. And most people didn't. She wasn't exactly everyone's cup of tea and she knew that. She just needed someone today. She needed someone who she thought might be kind to her and she had thought straight away of Julia. Julia was someone who had always been lovely whenever she had met her, even though she had never spent any length of time with her. Julia had kind eyes. Vic had also secretly—and not so secretly —crushed on Julia, of course she had; Julia was stunning, striking looking and always immaculately put together. She was so smart and so capable. Swoony-Julia. Swoolia.

There was a knock at her bedroom door.

Fuck.

"It's Julia, can I come in?"

Fuck.

"Just a minute." Vic grabbed an armful of the clothes scattered on her floor and shoved them inside the wardrobe and shut the door. It perhaps made the room look marginally better, but it still looked a mess. She pulled the curtains open, allowing the daylight in. It nearly blinded her and she blinked against the light.

Fuck.

Vic opened the door. "Um, hi. Come in."

God, I'm such a fucking moron.

Julia looked incredible in a dark red skirt suit and heels. She was taller than Vic with her heels on, but Vic decided without them they would be about the same height.

"Have a seat."

The only chair in the corner of the room was stacked high with clothes and bags and assorted other possessions. Vic watched as Julia scanned the room and decided upon the bed. She perched on the edge of the bed and Vic threw herself on the end of it.

"I make a great listener," Julia said kindly. "If you wanted to talk."

"I'm sorry, I shouldn't have called you. This really isn't your job."

"Please, Victoria. I'm happy to help. I have nothing on till Alexandra is back. And if you need more time, I'm sure the Princess will understand if we need to delay our meeting."

It felt as though Julia could sense there was something really wrong with her. Vic looked down at Julia's calf muscles, so lean and elegant in the heels. She looked down at her own legs in her scruffy jeans and odd socks. She wriggled her toes into the thick piled carpet.

She took a deep breath and tried to calm her heart rate.

"So, I have a thing at 1pm. An appointment. In London. And I don't want to go alone. But I told Princess and Bodyguard that I do want to go alone. But I don't actually want to go alone. And I actually have nobody else. And I don't want to ask Princess or Bodyguard, because they have their own *stuff* that makes this complicated." Vic picked the skin around her finger-

nails and her finger began to bleed. She
studied the blood carefully. She could see
Julia's lovely elegant feet in the heels out of
the corner of her eye. "So, I thought maybe
I could ask you. Stupid, I know. I shouldn't
have asked. You don't have to come. I know
you are really busy with important work."

"Of course I'll come with you. I have
nothing important on. My meeting with
Alexandra isn't until 4 and I can delay that
if necessary. She wouldn't mind. Come on,
let's get you a plaster for that finger and get
it cleaned up. Get some shoes on. I'll order
a car. We will need to get going to make it
on time."

Vic looked up at Julia who stood in
front of her and offered her a hand up. She
took Julia's perfectly manicured hand and
allowed herself to be pulled up. She moved
robotically to pull her dirty Nike's on.

Julia led her through the castle to a first
aid kit in an office downstairs. She took
Vic's hand tenderly and cleaned it with an
antiseptic wipe before applying an elasto-
plast where Vic had torn the skin off. Vic
felt safe with her.

Vic followed her out to the car.

Julia could have sat in the front with the driver, but she chose to sit in the back with Vic. Vic watched her elegant brown fingers and nude painted nails as they lay still in Julia's lap. Vic could never keep her own hands from fidgeting and pulling skin from each other particularly when she was nervous.

The first part of the journey was silent until Julia spoke eventually. "Do you want to talk about this appointment? Don't worry about the driver. He can't hear." Her voice was kind and nonjudgmental. Even so, Vic struggled to say the words.

"It's..." her voice faltered. "An abortion." Her voice was quiet.

She felt Julia's hand suddenly taking her own. Julia's hand was warm and soft. Vic looked up and Julia was looking in her eyes. "My darling, please don't worry. I'll never judge anything. I'll be here for you. Do you want me to come in with you?"

Vic felt herself starting to cry. "Yes," she murmured. "Please." Julia's arms reached for her and enveloped her into her warmth, pulling her close, and Vic let the tears overtake her. Julia rocked her as though she was a baby and Vic let herself fall apart against Julia's soft pillowy breasts.

The car ground to an eventual stop, and Vic knew she needed to stop crying and leave the safety of Julia's breast, but it just seemed like too big of a step.

It was Julia who pulled away slightly and handed a tissue to Vic. Vic noticed the damp patch on Julia's blouse where her tears had stained it and she felt guilty for bringing her messy self to ruin Julia's perfect image.

"My darling," Julia began. Vic liked the way Julia called her that. "Are you sure this is what you want to do? I promise you, I will hold your hand through it if you want to go ahead. But you can still change your mind if it isn't what you want."

Vic felt the tears drying on her cheeks.

Fuck, I'm such a mess.

"I don't know. I thought I did know. But I don't. It was an accident. A one-night stand. I'm just terrified of being a terrible mother, like my own mother was. I don't want to fuck it up." Vic focussed on the skin around an unbandaged fingernail and picked vigorously.

"Darling, it doesn't matter if you are a single mother. It doesn't matter if you aren't with the father. It doesn't matter if your own mother was terrible—you can learn, you can be so much better. You are an incredible woman, Victoria. You are capable of whatever you put your mind to. Women who win Olympic golds don't fuck things up."

Vic looked up at Julia.

She knows who I am. And, she said 'fuck'.

Vic smiled weakly. "I always thought you didn't even know who I was."

"I know who you are." Julia smiled back. "I watched your big win on television before I ever met you and I thought to myself, that is some awesome and capable woman right there."

Vic felt Julia's warmth rush through her. She put her hand to her belly and she felt the small bump. She did believe in abortion and a woman's right to choose. She did believe in it, but maybe this was her time to have a child. Maybe she could be the mother that Julia and Alex thought she could be. Maybe she could put her mind to it and do well at it.

"Do you want me to go in and cancel your appointment?" Julia asked her tenderly, as though her answer was what mattered, not Julia's own opinion or anyone else's.

Vic nodded and watched as Julia squeezed her hand then got out of the car and walked up the steps to the clinic.

She could do this. She could have a baby. She would keep this baby.

10

Alex looked up from the book she was reading about multiple pregnancies to see Vic entering the living area of the castle and Audrey got up to go to her. The sun was beginning to fall to signal the autumn evening.

Alex put down her book and got up to hug and console Vic. An abortion must be one of the most difficult things a woman could go through in her life. But she was surprised to see Vic looking lighter than she had in weeks and happy. Vic sat straight down on the floor with Audrey and kissed her on her big floppy lips and ruffled her ears.

"Are you... okay?" Alex asked cautiously.

"Never better," Vic replied in an upbeat voice. "So, I'm keeping the baby. I didn't go through with the abortion. So it seems your triplets are going to have a big sister."

Alex felt a smile spreading across her face as she met Vic's gaze. "Ah, Vic, a little girl! I'm so so happy for you. For all of us! I couldn't in fact be happier. I literally cannot believe we are going to have four babies soon! If everything goes well. Yours might end up being the little sister. Because apparently triplets come very early according to everything I am learning." Alex indicated the book.

Vic got up and picked Alex up in a hug. "We are going to be mums, Princess. We are going to be fucking mums! Can you believe it? I never ever imagined either of us would get here after our screwed up upbringings."

"Me either." Alex smiled wryly as Vic put her down. "It's like everyone thinks we must have had the perfect childhoods growing up with such privilege and wealth, and while so much of it was amazing—the places we grew up and the educations we were lucky enough to get—the actual parenting we received was abysmal and yours was downright neglectful. You were left alone so much in that big old house from when you were so very young. It is no wonder the dogs and horses are your best friends. At least I had nannies caring for me and taking the roles my parents had no interest in."

They sat down on the elaborate sofa.

"We are going to do it right, Princess. We are going to learn everything there is to know about being mums and we will help each other, right? We will give these babies the best future."

"We definitely will! Vic, what made you change your mind. Today, about the abortion. Where have you been? Did you go to the clinic?"

Vic went quiet for a minute before speaking.

"I did." She held a strand of her straw-coloured hair in her fingers and twirled it around her finger. "So, you know how I told you I wanted to go alone. I didn't really want to go alone. I just have this thing where I struggle to ask for help. I struggle to admit that I might ever need other people. I'm so used to being a lone wolf. I *thrive* on being a lone wolf. But this time...well, you guys had your own shit going on. So, I asked Julia to go with me."

"Julia? My Julia?" Alex raised her eyebrows in surprise.

"Yep, your Julia. Swoony-Julia. Swoolia." Vic screwed up her face a little and Alex knew she was just giving the nickname because Alex expected it. "I'm sorry. I wasn't a dick with her. I wasn't messing around. I just needed someone. I just needed not to be alone."

"Vic, it's okay." Alex reached over and put a hand on Vic's arm. "I'm not mad."

"She was so nice to me. So very kind. And by the time we got to the clinic, I just, well, I think I just realised I didn't actually want to go through with it. Maybe she helped me realise. She was so kind to me, Alex."

Alex couldn't remember the last time Vic had used her actual name instead of calling her *Princess*.

Alex squeezed her arm. "Julia is kind. She is awesome. I'm so happy she was there for you. I'm so sorry Erin and I didn't realise how much you were struggling. I hate that we weren't there for you. I should have been. What we are going through is so similar and yet so different, but it was selfish of me not to think of you. You are so strong, Vic. I always just think you can handle anything. I did know you hadn't been right lately. I should have been better at seeing through your facade and seeing the real you. I'm sorry."

"It's alright," Vic said. "I need to get better at asking for help."

"You do." Alex smiled.

"I know you told me ages ago about a psychotherapist you used to see who had helped you. I'm wondering if you could hook me up with her? There's stuff, you know, in my head. I know I'm not normal. I know I'm fucked up. I'm thinking maybe I could get help and start sorting my shit out before my baby is born. That way I'll be a better mum to her."

Alex smiled at her. "Of course. I'll introduce you to her." Alex had a thought.

"What's going to happen with your horses while you're pregnant?"

"Oh, I'll not stop riding. I'll just ride the ones I trust not to throw me off."

"So no riding Satan-the-leg-breaker?"

Vic laughed. "Well, no. I think that would probably be a bad plan. He can wait a few months. I don't want to have to re-name him Satan-the-baby-killer."

Alex made a face. "That's a sick joke, Vic."

Vic laughed. "Well, you know me."

"I do indeed. What are you going to do about the Duke of Leicester? Will you tell him?"

"Well, that is actually where I went this afternoon. Obviously, I didn't want to tell him, but I felt since I was actually going to have the child, he deserved to know."

"Oh wow, how did it go?"

"Well, he's still fucking annoying," Vic laughed. "But, he's in a new relationship with Lord Ashforth's daughter and he is desperate to marry her. She's like twenty years old and looks like a fucking model. Anyway, the point is, that he didn't care. He wants me to keep him out of it and not tell anyone so that Schoolgirl-Supermodel-Ashforth doesn't find out. So, that basically suits me *more* than fine. I mean, the sex was pretty good and he is hot. But he is *unbearably* posh. So, she is welcome to him. He offered to pay monthly for the kid and to keep me quiet, but I'm not bothered about that. I don't want his money. I'm just grateful that I'm not going to have to deal with him. He wants to have his lawyer draw up paperwork that signs away his parental rights in exchange for me keeping his name out of it."

"That's what you want?"

"Absolutely, nothing I want more now. You know me, I don't do relationships. I'm so happy to go it alone."

"In that case, I am really happy for you." Alex smiled. "And you are so right. He is really fucking annoying."

"THANKS FOR LOOKING after Vic yesterday. I should have been there for her and I wasn't." Alex sat down with Julia, and Jess rushed in with lunch for them both.

"No problem at all. Happy to be able to

help." Alex smiled at Julia noticing as she usually did, Julia's flawless skin.

"I know she's a little *eccentric?* Well, she's just Vic. I hope it wasn't too difficult." Alex always felt the need to apologise for Vic. She adored Vic, but she was well aware that not everyone appreciated her swearing and her lack of manners. Alex took a mouthful of Cajun chicken. Lunch was a tasty Cajun-crumbed chicken breast and salad. It was delicious.

"Victoria is actually incredible. Everything she has achieved on her own is so impressive. I watched the Olympics on TV when she won her gold medal. I'm in awe of her when I see her riding those difficult horses on the estate. Nothing scares her, does it? Sure, she needed a hand yesterday, but she has a real strength to her, a real fire. Please, don't feel the need to apologise for her."

Alex smiled. "That's Vic alright. No fear. The Lone Wolf. She is so talented with the horses, yes. You know she takes the horses other people won't these days? She takes the young ones, the difficult ones, the dangerous ones, and she tames them and trains them before selling them on?"

"I figured it was something like that. I've seen her going across that grass in front of the castle as though she was in a rodeo on that big brown horse. Whatever that horse did, Victoria wasn't going to be dislodged. She stayed calm, she stayed on the horse. She calmed him down. It was like horse magic to watch."

"For sure. She has such a way with animals." Alex ran her hand through her hair. "Anyway, I need to tell you the other news and get your advice. So, obviously you know I am pregnant. Well, the news that came as a shock to all of us is that it is triplets."

"Oh, Alexandra. Huge congratulations, that is incredible news." Julia smiled widely at Alex and her lipstick was perfect.

"Well, I mean it is incredible news and we are both obviously delighted. But there is a slight issue. We were advised that the pregnancy is very high risk. And because of who I am and who the potential child will be, we were advised to reduce the fetuses from three to one. Erin and I both agreed we cannot do that and we want to go ahead with the three of them and give them every chance at life. Dr. Keller is obviously an exceptional obstetrician and she has arranged for a multiple pregnancy specialist to be brought in too. I will see the specialist next week. I will give Dr. Keller permission to share my medical files with you. I'll need you to assess the risks we are dealing with and make a plan for when and how we announce the pregnancy publicly. What are your thoughts?"

Julia smiled empathetically at Alex as she finished a mouthful of food. "This is beautiful." She indicated with her fork. "I'm so sorry you and Erin have been through that decision on your own. I cannot imagine how hard it has been. You could have confided in me, you know?"

"I know. I nearly did, but I wanted us to make the decision for us. I didn't want us to hang our decision on *who I am.* This is about our babies, our future as a family. For once, I needed it not to be about me being a princess. Now we have decided what is best for us, the ball is in your court."

"Got it." Julia smiled confidently. "I will

discuss with Dr. Keller, but my initial thought is we give it a couple of weeks to see if we are still in the same situation and there have been no negative developments medically. But my instinct is that you speak openly to the press. You and Erin both do a television interview and you address everything from Nicolas as the donor to the difficult process you have been through so far and the perhaps difficult journey that lies ahead for you. Make yourselves human and the people will empathise and love you more for it. The people love you, Alex. This will just give them more to love. The risk you take is that the people will obviously need to know if things go wrong further down the line and if that does happen your pain would be public. How do you feel about it?"

"I'm not sure I have much choice. My life is public. I agree it is better to get the whole story out in our own words. I would always rather have a voice."

"And what a voice you do have. When you speak, people sit up and listen. Get out there, advocate for your decision, share your struggles and your advice." Julia was confident as usual, and Alex was confident that Julia was right. "I think you need to make it clear you were faced with an impossible choice. And you cast no judgement on people who would have taken the option of selective fetal reduction."

"I don't."

"I know that. We need to make sure everyone knows that and you remain everyone's favourite Princess. Alexandra the good."

Alex nodded. "Okay, I'm with you. Discuss with Dr. Keller. Plan the TV interview. I'm ready when you are."

THE NEXT COUPLE of weeks leading up to the TV interview were full of appointments with Dr. Keller and Dr. Farah Bryce, who was the multiple pregnancy specialist who had been flown in from the US to work with Dr. Keller and take care of Alex and the babies. Alex was really starting to notice a bump. She could almost feel the babies growing by the day and she felt a constant state of tiredness.

Alex figured Dr. Bryce to be mid-50s. She had salt and pepper hair and a certain butchness to her. She had strong capable hands and a sharp mind that Alex found reassuring. Alex trusted Dr. Keller when she said that Dr. Farah Bryce was the best in the world for multiple pregnancies.

Alex and Erin were in for a scan with the two of them when Dr. Bryce looked up and said, "So, there are no issues. The little one is still a bit small but no major concerns yet. Are the Royal power couple wanting to know the sex of these babies? Because I can tell you now if you want to know."

Alex and Erin looked questioningly at each other. With everything else that had been going on, the gender of the babies hadn't seemed like a priority and it wasn't something they had really decided on.

"What do you think?" Alex asked her.

"I'd like to know. In case. Well, in case anything happens. We can get to know the three of them individually and maybe name them. So we can be rooting for each one of them individually? I think that might be good. Dr. Bryce, would that work? Can we name them?"

"Sure you can!" Dr. Bryce was enthusiastic. "Make a pleasant improvement on me calling them A, B and C. Alexandra, would you like to know their genders?"

Alex nodded, it seemed like another step closer to them being real. "Yes, I would."

"So, see this one here?" She pointed at the monitor. "This is Baby A. She's the biggest. She is thriving. She is a girl."

Alex looked at Erin smiling. There were tears in Erin's eyes.

"See here—Baby B—Baby B is big too. Baby B is doing well. Baby B is a boy."

Alex felt overwhelmed with joy. She felt tears in her own eyes too.

"Baby C, right under here." Dr Bryce adjusted the transducer. "Baby C is the smallest. Baby C is the one most likely to run into problems. Baby C is a girl."

Alex felt Erin's hand on her belly and Erin's kiss on her forehead. It felt magical. Terrifying, but magical. Two girls and a boy.

This is my family now.

11

Erin couldn't stop thinking about two little girls and a little boy. She prayed with everything she had that they would all be okay. She had been at the stables with Shimmer late because they had got back late from the clinic. Erin did a lot of her processing and thinking in the peace and quiet of being around the horses or of riding on the estate. She couldn't stop thinking about her little family and how crazy it would be to suddenly have three babies all at once. Well, four, because Vic's little girl would be there too.

When she made it back home, Alex was

lying naked on their bed, reading. Her belly was growing by the day, her breasts were so much bigger, her areolas looked darker and her nipples were beginning to protrude more; her body was changing and Erin knew some level of change would be permanent. Erin knew it didn't matter how Alex's body changed, she would love her and desire her endlessly. Something about the swelling of Alex's breasts and belly was so womanly and so sexy. They hadn't had sex for a while, they had both been absorbed in worry and their own fears. Erin had worried about hurting Alex when her body had more important things to be focussing on. Erin had been so aware that Alex was constantly being poked and prodded and examined medically and she knew how fed up with it all Alex was. But she knew from the look in Alex's eyes as she put her book down that Alex was horny tonight.

"So, Sergeant Erin Kennedy, Princess of Scotland, Duke of Fife. I was wondering if you wanted to give Mrs. Kennedy an orgasm tonight? It has been a while and I'm feeling suddenly really in the mood!" Alex's eyes were sparkling like sapphires in the light from the lamp on the nightstand. She rolled onto her side and Erin noticed new roundness through her hips and how her bump and breasts dropped with gravity as she lounged. Her body looked golden in the light. Her hair fell loosely over her shoulder. She wore no makeup. Erin thought she had never seen anything more beautiful.

"Give me two minutes. I really need a shower. But then, I am all yours for whatever you want, Mrs. Kennedy."

Alex smiled seductively at her.

Erin stripped off her clothes and showered the smell of the stables from her body quickly, determined not to keep Alex waiting. She felt excited for the taste of Alex, excited to explore her changing body.

Erin dried herself quickly and headed back into the bedroom. She got onto the bed next to Alex and ran her hands down Alex's body watching the gooseflesh rise at her touch. Alex's body was still so responsive to her and she loved that. She ran her hand over Alex's breast and her nipple jumped in response to Erin's hand.

"Are they sensitive?" Erin asked.

"Yes, more so than usual, but in a good way, I think."

Erin felt suddenly desperate to have one of Alex's swollen nipples in her mouth. "You think I can suck it?"

Alex nodded and rolled onto her back to allow Erin access. Erin took Alex's big nipple into her mouth and it filled her mouth in a way it never had before. She ran her tongue around it, before suckling lightly, cautious not to cause Alex any pain. Alex moaned loudly. Erin ran her right hand down over Alex's belly and over the thick blonde patch of hair between her legs. She dipped her fingers lower, parting Alex's legs and slipping into a world of wetness. Alex felt even wetter than she ever had.

Erin played and teased with her fingers, sliding them up and down, casually moving from Alex's clitoris down her vulva to her anus and back again. Erin suckled her nipple gently and felt it swell further in her mouth.

Alex was going crazy next to her, her breathing quickening, her moans coming loud and often. Erin teased her for as long as she could bear before moving down and lying between Alex's legs, her mouth finding the places her fingers had just been. Alex's vulva, just like her nipples, was more swollen and pronounced than usual and absolutely soaking wet. Erin was amazed by the changes pregnancy had already brought to her body but this was still Alex, and those changes turned her on and made her only want her wife more. She absorbed herself in the taste of Alex, in taking Alex in her mouth and with her tongue. Her left hand was on Alex's hip as she felt Alex squirming and moaning and her right hand ran up over Alex's body leaving a trail of gooseflesh in its wake.

"Please..." Alex gasped.

Erin knew she wanted her fingers inside of her, but she was willing to wait and let Alex beg for it. She enjoyed hearing her beg.

Her voice was raspy. "Please... fuck me. I need to feel you inside me...."

Erin moved her right hand down between Alex's legs. She teased Alex with her fingers sliding up and down while she ran her tongue over Alex's clitoris.

"Please... please..." Alex asked again and Erin could deny her no more. She pushed her fingers inside of Alex, feeling her body open up to take them and Alex pushing her hips forwards craving more. Erin added another finger and Alex began to thrust against her fingers. Erin's mouth was on Alex's clit. It was seconds before Alex's orgasm overtook her and she gushed over Erin's hand and mouth. Her orgasm felt huge as she throbbed against Erin's fingers and she waited a little before she slowly slid her fingers out of her wife.

Alex's legs were shaking.

"Are you okay?" Erin asked.

"Yes. Will you lick me slowly? I think I can come again."

Erin didn't need asking twice. Her mouth moved straight back to Alex, her tongue moving in long slow strokes. It was barely a minute before a huge orgasm overcame Alex's body again, flooding Erin's face, Alex's whole body shuddering in the aftermath.

Erin laughed to herself. That was some

second orgasm. Alex lay in a daze, post-orgasm, and Erin wiped her face on the bedsheet before moving up the bed to take Alex in her arms and hold her.

"You've made a right mess of this bed, you know?"

Alex laughed. "I know. It felt like an eruption down there. I've never had an orgasm like it. Maybe pregnancy is doing good things to my body? That was fucking incredible."

"I'll say," Erin laughed. "Remind me to get a towel next time. Or two towels."

Alex laughed again. "Can we talk about baby names?"

"Now?!" Erin wasn't sure why she was ever surprised by Alex anymore. "Sure, we can talk about anything you like, Mrs. Kennedy."

"So, obviously, we can't go too wild on naming future members of the Royal Family. But I do want them to have individual names. This might be dumb, but I read the book, *Matilda*, when I was a kid and I always thought she was just the most amazing girl. I always wanted to have a little girl and call her Matilda."

Erin smiled as Alex nuzzled in under her arm and threw her left leg over Erin. "I loved Matilda. For sure. That is one name sorted. Baby A?"

"Yes, I was thinking Matilda is Baby A. Strong and doing well."

"Okay, Princess Matilda, it is. How about Baby B?" Erin didn't have strong feelings on baby names, but she knew that Alex would have.

"So, this is maybe a bit off the wall and feel free to say no."

"Go for it, Mrs. Kennedy."

"So, I know that Nicolas was very close to his grandfather whose name was Frank. He hasn't asked for this at all, but seeing as Baby B is going to be the only boy in the family, I was thinking maybe going to Nicolas's roots would be good. So he doesn't feel alone."

"Prince Frank, it is."

Alex smiled and sat up. "You really don't mind? You are happy with Matilda and Frank?"

Erin looked up at her wife and felt full of love. "I really don't mind. I really don't have any ideas. I'm not sure baby naming is my thing. I can't even name dogs and horses, I'm hopeless with ideas. I think it's nice too. I think little Frank should have a good link with Nicolas. Well, I think they all should. But Frank really is going to be surrounded by women. Incredible women, yes, but women all the same." Erin reached her arms above her head and stretched. "How about Baby C?"

"Florence," Alex said instantly. "It means 'to flourish and blossom.' I have every hope that Baby C will flourish and blossom."

"Princess Florence. Princess Matilda. Prince Frank. I wonder which one will come first? I wonder which one will be the future monarch?"

"In my head, it's Matilda. You just assume Baby A will come first, right? But it probably won't happen like that, will it?"

"I think anything could happen. But through it all, whatever happens, we have each other. Florence, Matilda and Frank have us both fighting for them."

"Lucky babies," Alex said.

"Lucky babies, indeed."

12

The interview on TV with Britain's most famous chat show host went well. People all around the world watched Alex and Erin's vulnerability as they spoke about their journey to start a family. There were tears in Alex's eyes as she spoke about the decision they had had to make and Erin knew they were real. The reaction from the public was overwhelmingly positive as they spoke openly about their excitement at the pregnancy and their fear that things might go wrong. Alex had spent years building favour with the media and even her coming out hadn't dulled her shine. Princess Alexandra was their golden girl. The People's Princess. The Royal that everyone knew and loved.

They had chosen to keep the babies' names to themselves for now. It was something personal they had just between them.

They had posed for a photoshoot for a glossy magazine, showing off Alex's bump. It was what the people wanted to see and Julia had encouraged them to do it. Alex hadn't really wanted to, she often found pregnancy photos to be cheesy, and she was struggling to come to terms with the changes to her body herself.

That evening after they had done the photoshoot, Erin had taken photos of her nude in their bedroom. It was Erin who made her feel beautiful again, as though she was the most beautiful woman in the world, even though her breasts and her belly were so much bigger than they ever had been. Alex had found it the most erotic thing, posing nude for Erin. She had felt the desire in Erin's eyes as she directed her and photographed her in the soft golden lamplight. The photos were carefully kept between the two of them, and when Alex looked at them, she could almost see what Erin saw. She did look beautiful and maternal in a way that she had never imagined.

VIC'S PREGNANCY progressed without complication over the winter and even though she due any day now, you could barely tell she was pregnant if you hadn't already known. Vic was cruising through it. She was still riding and teaching and rolling around on the floor with dogs and nothing had really changed for her.

Alex, on the other hand, was beginning to really struggle as the weeks went on. Her whole body and face felt ridiculously swollen. She was glad she had had the photos taken when she did, if she had waited any longer, she would not have looked "hot" pregnant, she would have looked like a big blob on short legs. She couldn't get used to the sheer size of her body. She was also glad it was winter and the weather was cold. She would never have survived in the heat. She was nearly 33

weeks now and Doctor Bryce had scheduled a C-section for 34 weeks. They were
hoping Alex's body would hold on to them
until then and not go into labour any earlier—Florence needed all the time she
could get inside of Alex to give her the best
possible chance of survival, but at the same
time, Alex would be at risk if they let the
pregnancy go on too long. Alex was having
high blood pressure issues that she knew
the doctors were concerned about even
though they were trying desperately not to
stress her. Matilda and Frank continued to
do well. Florence was still small. Alex knew
the doctors didn't have high hopes for Florence's survival, they didn't say as much but
they always focussed on their hopes for
Matilda and Frank. Alex tried not to think
of the worst, tried not to think of anything
bad happening to Florence. She thought all
the time of good things, positive thoughts,
three little babies in her arms, three little
children running round. Florence, a lovely
little girl with blonde hair and bright blue
eyes sitting in the grass making daisy
chains. She knew Erin was doing the same.

They were both thinking good thoughts for Florence.

Nicolas had been supportive throughout the pregnancy from a distance. She sensed that he was trying desperately not to overstep. He cared, but he knew they weren't actually his children and she wasn't actually his wife.

THE KING HAD ASKED for a meeting with Alex and Julia and he came to meet Alex at the castle. She wasn't planning to leave the castle until it was time to go to the hospital. She had had these romantic dreams of a home birth in a pool of water, but as soon as *High-Risk Pregnancy* was declared, she knew she had no chance. The doctors weren't prepared to discuss any other birth plan than a scheduled C-Section and as Alex was determined to give each of her babies the best chance possible, she agreed to it.

Alex had always had a distant relationship with her father. She loved him and she felt that he loved her. As a child she had been brought up by nannies and then she was at boarding school, so she rarely spent time with her father or mother.

"Julia, hey." Alex smiled at Julia as she entered the room. "I would get up, but..." She pointed to her belly.

"No problem, Mama." Julia bent down and kissed Alex's cheek before sitting down. "I just had a message from His Majesty's security team. He should be with us any minute."

"Perfect," Alex said. Erin was out with the horses. Vic had stopped riding finally, because she was literally due any day, but she was still teaching Erin and Shimmer, who was back in good form, getting ready for the upcoming season.

Alex was shocked when she saw her father. It was the first time she had seen him since before they went to Scotland and he had changed so much in that time. She also realised she hadn't seen public appearances from him for a bit. He looked thinner and he looked grey in both skin and hair. So, when he began to speak, his words were no great surprise to Alex.

"Alexandra." He followed up her name

with a bout of coughing. He sat down in the biggest chair in the room. "I'm not a well man. I have cancer and my days are numbered. I don't know how long it will be, but you will become Queen sooner than perhaps later. If the doctors are right, within the next couple of months." He spoke matter-of-factly and without emotion in the same way he had approached everything Alex's whole life.

"Father, I'm so sorry. I... I don't know what to say." Alex felt a pit of emotion somewhere deep inside her, a grief for knowing she was going to lose the man who had supported her finally in these last few years. "How long have you known?"

"I've had the cancer for a few years now. They have only recently decided that it's going to finish me off imminently and I am not wanting treatment to prolong things. I'm wanting to take death on my own terms at home in my own bed. My own fault, one might say. The cigarettes, the alcohol."

"That's not what I'm thinking. Thank you. Thank you for blessing my coming out, my marriage, for giving us titles, for helping us to split from the church, for making my passage to becoming monarch so much smoother than it otherwise might have been."

"You've been a good girl, Alexandra. You always have. Your mother was always too hard on you, but I knew you would be the best heir I could hope for. I knew you were the one that would take this country forwards. The people adore you. You are what the country needs. Not some stuffy old fool like me." He coughed again. "Nobody knows yet. By the way. I'm not planning to announce it, I'm just wanting to die privately and surprise everyone. I'm wanting to wait out and see these babies though first, by the way." He smiled and his leathery old face creased up. Alex smiled.

"I can't believe I'm having three."

He laughed. "Do we have names?"

"I mean, I've got ideas. There's names we are calling them at the moment, but I know that you would need to authorise them before they are named officially."

"Of course, Alexandra. Go for it."

"Well, the two bigger ones are Matilda and Frank. Then there's the little one that I don't think the doctors have high hopes for. Her name is Florence."

The King smiled widely and Alex saw what she thought was pride in his eyes.

"I shall authorise those names here and now if those are what you want. Princess Matilda, Prince Frank and little Princess Florence. I'll be praying for Florence, Alexandra."

"Thank you, Father. Is there anything you want? Anything I can do?"

"Look after this country for me. Be the best monarch you can be. There is nothing else I need. And, I'm sorry about your mother, Alexandra. Don't ever let her win."

"What do I need to do?"

"You don't need to worry about anything now, Alexandra. My people will brief Julia on everything there is to know. Then, when it is time, she will tell you what you need."

Alex felt suddenly childlike and faint. Losing her father felt suddenly huge and overwhelming and she didn't know if she could survive it.

"Anyway." He stood up huffing and puffing. "Lovely to see you. I must go now."

As was typical of him, he walked out. He would always talk about facts, he never showed emotion. Alex felt shellshocked and she felt her heartbeat racing.

Tears began to fall from her eyes. She watched as Julia called Erin immediately and also Dr. Keller and then she sat next to Alex and put her arm around her.

"Hey, hey, come here. I know it was a shock. I'm not sure he has chosen the best way or time of breaking that news, but I can only assume it was something he needed to do." Julia held Alex as she cried.

"I don't even know why I'm crying. We have never been close. But I just can't help it. I feel like I should go and stay with him, be with him for his last weeks or months or whatever there is."

"Alex, he hasn't asked you for that and it isn't your duty. You have your own family to worry about now and he knows that. He isn't asking you for that. He is asking you to step up to the role you have been prepared for all your life. You will be Queen soon."

Alex began to sob. "Oh god, I'm not ready. Not like this. I thought I would be older. I thought I would have more time.

Just to be, to learn to be a mother. To look after my children. I don't want it. I don't want to be Queen."

Alex felt her breathing quicken and she started to panic. Her breaths couldn't come quickly enough. "Oh god."

At that moment Erin and Vic rushed in and Erin immediately sat the other side of her and Alex collapsed into her arms struggling to breathe.

"I'm calling Dr. Keller," Vic announced.

"I already did," Julia said.

"Why isn't she fucking here? I'm calling her again," Vic said, impatiently striding up and down the room. She looked lean all over apart from her belly that sprung out from her looking like it was fake and strapped on to her.

Alex watched as Erin's eyes darted round the room; clearly, she was deciding that Vic was stressful to have around.

"I'm going to take Alex into the bedroom, maybe run her a bath, try and help her stay calm, okay?"

Erin took Alex's arm and helped her up. She felt stupid that she could barely even get up herself now. "Hey, Lex, look at me. Calm down. Stay calm. It's okay."

"It's not okay. He's dying. I, uh... I don't know what to do."

"Baby, there's nothing you can do. Nothing any of us can. He needed to tell you himself, but you can't go and care for him. Not now. Look at you. Our babies need you."

"I can't become Queen. I'm not ready." Alex felt the room start to close in on her as Erin sat her down on the bed.

"Lex, you have been ready for this moment your whole life. You are the most capable woman I have ever met. You can do this...when it is time. It isn't time yet. You can do anything. I believe in you and I am right here with you. Breathe slowly. Breathe with me."

Erin positioned her on the bed and took deep breaths with Alex, slowly counting her through them. Alex felt calmer in herself but she couldn't help the fear that was bubbling up deep inside. Fear of losing her father and fear of the immense level of responsibility that came with that. Sure, she had been prepared for this moment her whole life. But now that it was approaching, it seemed like the biggest, most insurmountable thing in the world. Alex closed her eyes and wanted everything to go away.

13

Vic was still pacing in the living room when Julia put a hand on her arm. "Hey, Victoria. Steady. Calm down. It's okay. It will be okay."

Vic felt electricity run through her from where Julia's hand had touched her. Her eyes met Julia's.

"I just... I'm just worried about Princess. She's always so calm. So if she's having a breakdown, it must be fucking bad. I know how complex and distant her relationship with her father has always been, but I know deep down she has always had this immense love and respect for him. I just think, it's complicated for her, you know.

Losing the King is a helluva complication for her."

Vic felt a sudden urge to bury herself in Julia's arms and in her breasts again like she did on that day in the car at the clinic. Julia was wearing a nude-coloured blouse and a pencil skirt, and Vic thought she had never seen a woman more attractive and put together. Her dark hair was pinned up neatly.

She snapped out of her thoughts quickly when she felt a sharp pain in her belly. "Fuck," she said loudly.

"What is it?" Julia looked concerned.

"Oh, nothing, most likely. I just felt a pain. Like period pain."

"Like a contraction?"

"It had better fucking not be! I haven't got time to have a baby right now."

"I'm going to call the midwife just in case. Dr. Keller is coming anyway for Alexandra so she can look at you too. I'll get Jess to organise filling up the birthing pool."

Vic had been keen from the start to have her baby at the castle. She wanted as little to do with hospitals as was possible. She had had the bare minimum of scans and luckily her pregnancy had been straightfor-ward in every way, so Dr. Keller had been happy with the home birth plan. So long as she was prepared to change it if there were any concerns. On her examination with Dr. Keller a couple of days ago, the baby had been in the perfect position and ready to go. She had worried it would upset Alex, her having a home birth, because she knew it would have been what Alex wanted if she had had any choice in the matter. But Alex had actually been hugely supportive and organised for her to have a birthing pool delivered and set up in a lovely room filled with light on the south side of the castle.

"Just because I have to have a surgery and a million doctors doesn't mean you can't have a beautiful birth, Vic." Alex was keen to give Vic everything she couldn't have, and Vic thought again how lucky she was to have a friend like Alex. No expense had been spared in planning the perfect birth for Vic.

Vic watched as Julia made the phone calls.

Swoolia. She is so hot.

She felt another sharp pain. *Oh god. Maybe it really is coming. I definitely didn't do enough preparation for this.*

As Julia got off the phone, the door opened and Dr. Keller walked in. She was as immaculate as always. Vic was wearing yoga pants and a scruffy T-shirt that was stretched over her bump and she suddenly felt like such a mess in front of Julia and Dr. Keller.

"Dr. Keller. Thanks for coming out," Julia was immediately professional. "So, Alexandra is resting now. She seems calmer, but we would definitely like you to take a look at her. She has had a big shock. But meanwhile..."

As if on cue Vic heard herself yelp like a kicked dog as another powerful wave of pain ran through her.

"I think Victoria might be having contractions." Dr. Keller nodded and looked Vic up and down. "How long have these contractions been happening?"

"Not sure, half an hour?"

"How close together?"

"I don't fucking know! Maybe five minutes?"

"Right, I think you have some time. I'm going to go and check on Alexandra and if you could strip off your bottom half and try to stay comfortable, I'll examine you when I get back." Dr. Keller was as efficient as ever as she breezed through to Alex and Erin's bedroom.

Vic felt awkward suddenly. Was she just supposed to start getting undressed in front of Julia?

Suddenly Julia walked across the room to her with her hips swaying and she handed a folded clothing item to Vic.

"So, I didn't want to overstep, but I bought this for you, for your labour. It might feel comfortable. No pressure at all, I won't feel offended if you don't wear it."

Vic took it and held it up. It was a big, loose-fitting, blue-grey nightgown with buttons down the front. It looked like it would reach nearly to her knees. She felt a wave of gratitude, swiftly followed by another contraction. She gripped her stomach for a second. "Thank you. So much. Honestly, this looks perfect."

Julia smiled. "I'll give you a minute to change. I'll go check in with Jess to see what else is going on." Julia left the room and Vic swiftly changed into the nightgown. It felt loose around her body and covered her up and that was just what she needed. She knew this labour thing would probably take hours and hours. She couldn't believe Julia had sorted it for her. Was that part of Julia's job?

When Dr. Keller arrived, she was closely followed by Erin and a waddling fat little Alex wearing a loose summer dress. Every bit of Alex, including her face, looked unnaturally swollen. Vic couldn't get over how big Alex had suddenly become in the past couple of weeks. She had no idea how her tiny frame was managing to carry three babies.

Vic felt another wave of pain run through her and each time felt worse. "Ugh," she grunted. "I've changed my mind. I regret deciding to give birth naturally. Get me to hospital, give me *all* the drugs and do some fucking surgery, Dr. K."

"Right, Victoria. Lie back on this sofa and let me have a feel for your cervix. We need to know what is going on down there."

Vic felt another powerful contraction go through her. "Fuck me. Is it just me, or are these contractions supposed to be like this?" Ugh. "I feel like I need to push."

Dr. Keller remained calm as she inserted her fingers to study Vic's cervix. "Okay, so don't panic, but your cervix is well dilated already. I think you may be experiencing precipitous labour."

"Preci—what? What the fuck is that?"

"Basically means fast labour. I think your baby is coming quickly. Is the midwife here? I'd like to move you to the pool."

Julia's voice came from the doorway. Vic felt instantly calmed hearing her. "Midwife and pool are ready."

"Is this bad? This precipi-quick labour?" Vic felt a wave of panic and further pains of contractions.

"Normally, no. Some women's bodies just move faster than others. It will still most likely take a couple of hours. We have Entonox there for you for pain relief."

Vic felt herself swept through to the birthing pool room where the midwife awaited. Everything felt in a blur. "Where is the fucking pain relief?"

She was handed a plastic mouthpiece to suck on.

"See here, form a seal with your mouth and take deep slow breaths on it when you feel a contraction starting."

"So, like all the fucking time, then," Vic said drily and took a deep breath of the Entonox. She felt gradually hazy and less pain. After a minute, she felt a little high.

"This is like poppers," she declared loudly.

"Poppers?" asked Dr. Keller.

"They sell them in tiny glass bottles in gay clubs. You sniff them and they make you feel exactly like this. Like you are floating."

Dr Keller laughed heartily.

"Trust you to know that." Alex's voice was there.

"Right, Victoria, let's get you undressed and into this pool," the midwife suggested as Vic drowned the contractions in the sucking of the gas.

Vic unbuttoned the nightgown and stripped it off and got into the pool pretending to swim in it. "I'm naked, like a baby."

God, I feel so high.

"Fuck, is Swoolia here? She shouldn't see me like this. *Very* undignified." Vic sucked more on the plastic tube. She felt amazing. The voices of everyone seemed surreal.

"Swoolia?" Dr. Keller sounded confused.

"She means Julia."

"Why does she call me Swoolia?"

"SHHHHHHH!" Vic said loudly. "She must never ever know. Never ever know. Juliaaaa Swooliaaaaa."

"Vic, do you want us in here?" It was Erin's voice.

"Nah, I'm not bothered. You can wait outside if you like. I'm doing *fine*." Vic laid her head back in the water and tried to find a good position. Was this it? Was she really having a baby here?

14

A lex was trying to relax in the living room with Erin while they waited for news on Vic. Julia was moving between the two rooms keeping them updated and apparently holding Vic's hand when she needed it. Alex thought again how valuable Julia was to all of them.

Alex felt so grateful to have Julia, and of course, Erin. Always Erin. Her wife. There for her always. Alex jumped when she heard her mobile ring. It was on the table and Erin went to fetch it for her.

Erin looked surprised. "It's your mother."

Alex felt a wave of panic rush through

her. What on earth did her mother want?
They hadn't spoken since Cecilia had
threatened Erin last year before their wedding. Alex never wanted to speak to her
again. But here was her phone flashing
with her mother's name.

"You don't need to speak to her, you
know." Erin put her hand on Alex's arm.

"It might be important. With everything
that is going on." Alex made a swift decision and pressed *Accept*.

"Alexandra."

"Mother." Alex was cautious and felt
anxiety running through her body again.

"I've been informed about your father."
There was a moment of silence where Alex
felt it all over again. That visit from her father. That information that she still could
barely process.

"I want to implore you to step down
from the line of succession. Speak to the
King before he dies. You can step out of the
line of succession and then Arthur will take
the crown. You are no Queen, Alexandra.
You know that as well as I do. You have
made your life choices to pursue your own
disgusting lifestyle and to get yourself preg-

nant in a laboratory with someone who is not your husband. This is *not* the behaviour of a Queen. These children will be illegitimate bastards, you of all people should know that. We will fight legally for them to be removed from the line of succession. Take the noble decision and remove yourself now before the King dies."

Alex felt tears welling up. She felt sick and in pain. She needed to summon strength from somewhere to stand up to her mother.

She took a deep breath. "My love is valid. My marriage is valid. My children are valid heirs to the throne. I will always fight for what is good and right. Take your campaign of hate elsewhere and stay well away from my children. You may have spent a lifetime trying to break me, but I will never allow you anywhere near my children."

There was another moment of silence and Alex took a deep breath. It had taken everything she had to fight her mother.

"If they survive." Cecilia spoke with venom dripping from her voice.

"What?" Alex said in shock.

"*If* the babies survive. God's will might

be that they don't. God doesn't agree with your *disgusting* choice of lifestyle. God does not agree with how these children have been created and God has the power to take them away from you."

Alex felt herself crumbling and she threw the phone onto the floor and put her head in her hands. Tears overcame her. How could anyone say something like that? How could her own mother say that about her grandchildren?

"Florence..." Alex sobbed, and Erin immediately held her. "Cecilia thinks Florence will die..." Alex couldn't stop the sobbing. All she could think about was the little blonde girl that she dreamed of when she thought of Florence. The little girl that she was terrified of losing.

Erin held her and rocked her. "I've got you, Lex. I've got all of you. Florence will be alright. Everyone will be alright."

Alex thought about her mother's request. Should she step down from the line of succession? Should she go to her father and ask for that? She didn't feel ready to be Queen. Maybe this way she would never have to be. She could live an ordinary life with Erin and her babies and never have to be Queen.

What on earth should I do?

As she was thinking, Alex felt a sharp stab of pain in her belly and she cried out.

"Lex, are you okay? What is it?"

She felt a rush of something between her legs and felt suddenly soaking wet right through her underwear and her dress. She reached up under her dress. As she pulled her hand away, she saw the blood. Lots of blood. It was then that she began to truly panic.

15

Erin ran to the birthing pool room where Vic was still in labour and Julia was kneeling next to her, holding her hand.

"Bodyguard..." Vic drawled, still high. "Swoolia is looking after me, not to worry."

"Dr. Keller. Come quickly, it's Alex."

Dr. Keller clearly recognised something in Erin's face and got up quickly and was right behind Erin as they burst into the living room. She took one look at the blood all over Alex's lemon yellow dress and the sofa.

"Get a car. Hospital. Right now! Can you carry her?"

"Yes." Erin didn't take a second to think twice. She would get Alex to the elevator and get her out to the cars.

"*Jess!*" Erin caught herself screaming. There was no time to waste. Jess came running into the room. "Get a driver ready. Right now. And get me someone to help carry Alex." Jess bolted out of the room to do Erin's bidding. Dr. Keller was on the phone to what Erin assumed was the hospital. Erin was helping Alex off the sofa when Joanne Davis, Alex's bodyguard, rushed in. Joanne had had time off and an easy time of it towards the end of Alex's pregnancy when she hadn't left the castle. Joanne had come back for birth preparations and she was more than ready now.

"Alex, one arm round my shoulder, one arm around Joanne and we are going to lift you and get you out to the car fast."

Alex nodded numbly and reached her arms up for the shoulders of her two tall, strong bodyguards. They each lifted one of her legs and started moving quickly towards the elevator. There was a lot of blood on Alex's yellow dress. Erin wasn't squeamish, but this was Alex and her babies and although she didn't know a huge amount about pregnancy this blood had to be bad. Plus, she had seen the look on Dr. Keller's face and that was when she really knew it was bad.

They soon had Alex out of the elevator and into the back of the Range Rover and Erin could see straight away that the driver wasn't wasting time. Erin and Dr. Keller were in the back with Alex and Joanne Davis was in the front with the driver.

Dr. Keller took a moment to feel for Alex's cervix and Erin watched as she screwed up her face slightly and when she removed her hand it was covered in blood.

She moved her hands, touching Alex's abdomen. "Does it hurt?"

"Yes," Alex gasped.

Dr. Keller reached into the bag she had brought with her and brought out three monitors. Erin had no idea how she was managing to work in such limited space as the Range Rover moved so fast. She shoved Alex's dress up above the bump and got to work attaching the monitors. Soon Alex had an assortment of discs stuck to her belly and Dr. Keller was studying the monitors.

"We have three heartbeats," she announced confidently.

Alex moaned and her face screwed up with pain. "I'm scared," she whispered. Erin's arm was around her shoulder and with her other arm she held Alex's hand. She kissed her hair. "I've got you. I'm with you. I promise."

Dr. Keller got on speakerphone with Dr. Bryce.

"Driver, how long?" Dr. Keller called to the front of the vehicle.

"Ten minutes," came the response.

"Right, ETA is ten minutes. I think we have placental abruption. Prep for emergency C-Section. I still have three heartbeats but babies are in distress and so is the Princess."

Erin felt scared, but she was someone who knew how to deal with fear. As a bodyguard, not dissimilar to a doctor, that's what you do. You take a deep breath and swallow any fear or panic. You stay calm and you deal with the drama, the danger, whatever the situation is. She felt futile here though.

All of her skills and training was useless now. Alex looked suddenly very pale. Dr. Keller's face looked suddenly very serious. Erin felt sick to her very core and kissed Alex's hair again. "I've got you, Baby. I've got you."

A HOSPITAL TROLLEY bed waited outside the hospital doors. There had been emergency plans all along and Royal births took place in the VIP section of the hospital on a separate wing with its own entrance. The drivers and security and hospital staff had all done practice runs in case of an emergency, and here was that emergency exactly, and everyone moved like they were in a well-rehearsed dance. Except for Erin. She suddenly felt like she had no place in it. Hospital staff lifted Alex from the car to the bed and started wheeling her straight through the double doors. Erin ran after them, like she might lose Alex if she wasn't fast enough. She knew this was the moment. Dr. Keller had briefed her before on how badly things might go wrong for both the babies and for Alex. What if Alex died in surgery? What if she never saw her again?

They had stopped in a room and were cutting Alex's dress from her with scissors. They threw a thin gown over her and she was surrounded by people doing things to her. Dr. Bryce had warned them that there would be a team of doctors. One for each baby and both her and Dr. Keller for Alex. There were also nurses, midwifes, anaesthetists. There were so many people. Erin had no idea who anyone was. They were all communicating with numbers and medical terms. Erin couldn't understand what they were saying.

"Right, get her into the OR, move fast. I'm scrubbing in." Dr Bryce seemed to be in charge.

Erin sat quietly in the corner of the room. She knew they had to do their job. She was determined not to be the kind of dramatic partner that hindered the medics.

The midwife, Josie, nodded to Erin. "You can speak to her quickly, before she goes to theatre."

Erin moved quickly to Alex's bedside.

Alex looked dazed and Erin wondered what they had given her. She looked really unwell. Erin was terrified and didn't know what to say.

"I love you, Lex. I'll be right outside."

"Make sure they save my babies. Make sure they fight for Florence, won't you? Florence can't die. She can't."

"I'll make sure." Erin was crying as she gripped Alex's hand and kissed her forehead.

I can't lose her. Not like this.

Alex's bed started moving as they took her away.

Erin felt Alex's hand slip from her fingers and she called after Dr. Bryce. "You heard her, Dr Bryce. Fight for Florence. It's the one thing she wants."

They had discussed with Erin before that if the C-section was an emergency that she wouldn't be allowed in theatre with them and they would be putting Alex under a general anaesthetic to do the surgery.

Erin sat back in the room that was now empty. She felt painfully alone. Joanne Davis came in to sit with her.

Josie, the midwife, bustled in and sat next to them both.

"Okay, so the bleeding is what we call a placental abruption. It is where one of the placentas has detached from the uterus wall, and we are concerned that the baby isn't getting enough oxygen. There is a risk to the Princess from the blood loss. There is a huge risk to the baby concerned and the other two babies are in distress too."

Erin looked up at Josie and saw the concern on her face. "It's Florence, isn't it? The baby with the placental abruption."

She knew the birthing team all knew the babies by both their letter and their name now. Josie nodded. "Yes, it is. Baby C. Florence."

"Will she be okay? Please, be honest with me."

"The doctors will do everything they can. You have the very best doctors in the world working on your wife, I promise you that."

"That isn't an answer. What do you think? Honestly. Please tell me."

Josie sighed deeply. "Honestly, Florence is small and that only makes her fight so much harder and that is before the placental abruption. I think you should prepare yourself that she might not make it."

Erin felt tears running down her face. She thought about what Cecilia had said to Alex on the phone about God taking her babies away from her. Alex's panicking about becoming Queen. Alex's fear of losing her father. Every cruel word her mother had ever said to her. It was all wrapped up in Florence. Alex needed Florence to live.

"Please, you don't understand how much Florence means to Alex. Please, go and tell them. If we lose Florence, it will break Alex."

Erin felt herself falling apart.

Josie nodded and headed out of the room. "I'll be back to update you," she called.

"I don't think I can just wait here," Erin called. "Please, can I come with you? I'll won't be any trouble."

Josie looked back at her and waited a moment.

"Okay, there's a viewing gallery for the OR. That's where I'm going. You can come.

We can hear the surgeons and see what is going on from up there."

Erin followed Josie quickly and entered a room with a big window looking down at the surgeons working.

Josie buzzed through to the OR and spoke on the intercom: "Sergeant Kennedy has impressed upon me the Princess's wishes that you do everything you can for Baby C. The Princess has a strong attachment to Florence."

Dr. Bryce answered, "Absolutely. I'm doing my best, but I'm not a magician. I think the best we can hope for is to save A and B now."

There were three incubators and small tables set up ready for each baby. Three medics at each table. Then there was Alex unconscious and a vibrant red slice to her big belly with Dr. Bryce's hands inside of her. Erin tried to detach and not look at Alex's face.

Suddenly a blood-covered, blue-looking baby was pulled out. It was small, barely filling Dr. Bryce's cupped hands "She's not looking good." Erin heard the call from Dr. Bryce. The doctor from one of the incubators took the baby immediately and someone snipped the cord.

"Florence?" Erin asked Josie cautiously.

"Yes," Josie said.

Florence was put on her own table and she was eerily quiet and still.

"Starting CPR, Baby C not breathing," the doctor called.

Erin felt tears flooding from her eyes. Florence was going to die.

"Let's move fast," Dr. Bryce said. "There is no way I'm losing all three of these. Dr. Keller. Help me in here."

Erin shook with fear.

"Okay, there's a lot of blood here. Princess is haemorrhaging. I need these babies out *right now* so I can save the mother."

Dr. Keller suddenly pulled out a baby. This one was bigger and more of a purple colour. "Baby A." Matilda was taken from her straight away and moved to her table with her own doctors. Within seconds, Matilda was crying. Definitely breathing. "Baby A breathing. Initial signs are good."

Erin glanced over to Florence's table. They were still doing CPR. She caught the eyes of Florence's doctor. He looked young, but he looked focussed.

It seemed like seconds before Frank was out and crying too. "Baby B breathing. Initial signs look good."

Florence was still silent. Erin noticed every doctor in the room kept glancing at her table.

Please save Florence. You have to save Florence.

Time felt like it was standing still.

Dr Bryce looked more serious than she ever had as her hands worked quickly and she snapped at her assistants.

"I will *not* have the future Queen of Great Britain bleeding out on my table. Oh no, not today."

Matilda and Frank were soon in their incubators and wheeled out of the room.

Erin felt Josie's hand on her arm. "You want to go and see them? You can see them now. They will go to the Princess's room. We have created a mini Neonatal intensive care unit in there specially."

Erin was frozen to the spot. "I can't leave Florence. I can't leave Alex."

They can't die. They can't.

16

Alex opened her eyes and felt dazed.

Erin was the first thing she saw. Her body felt somehow empty as though something was missing and then she remembered. The emergency surgery.

"My babies..." She tried to sit up and couldn't. She felt a sharp pain. "Are they okay?"

Erin held her hand. "They are all okay, Lex. Not out of the woods yet. They are in these little incubators. See here."

Alex felt tears pricking her eyes as she looked across at them.

My babies.

"Florence?" she asked.

"Florence is a fighter." Dr. Bryce's voice was loud and confident. "Florence is a tough little survivor. She wasn't breathing when she came out. It took eight minutes of CPR to resuscitate her. If I'm honest, I didn't rate her chances. She weighs less than 3lbs. We also nearly lost you. You haemorrhaged and lost a lot of blood. But sometimes miracles do happen. Someone was on your side in a big way today. You are lucky to be alive, and so is Florence, Ma'am."

Alex felt hazy and in disbelief. "Thank you. Thank you so much."

"We need to monitor them carefully the next few days particularly. But, aside from the usual concerns with a premature birth and also Florence's small size and the trauma she has been through, it all looks hopeful."

THE KING VISITED them the next day. He looked terrible. "I prayed for her, you know. I prayed for Florence."

"I think it might have worked, Father."

He squeezed her hand. "You will be an incredible Queen, you know. The country is lucky to have you."

He coughed loudly and Alex saw blood in his handkerchief.

"Which one was born first?" he asked, and Alex realised she hadn't even thought about that.

"It was Florence," said Erin.

"Then Princess Florence will be the next heir to the throne." He spoke confidently, and Erin and Alex looked at each other and smiled.

"I have everything in place," he said. "There is no doubt about the legitimacy of your children and their rightful positions in the line of succession. Don't let anyone scare you with that. Everything has been done legally. You'll be alright, Alexandra."

His eyes were kind, and she wondered about the relationship they might have had, could have had, if things had been different. She wondered about the relationship he might have had with the triplets if he survived long enough. But when he left her hospital room, it was as if they both knew it was the last time.

V<small>IC HAD GIVEN</small> birth quickly and easily to a healthy baby girl in the birthing pool. She FaceTimed Alex and Erin the following day.

"What's her name?" asked Alex.

"Hyzenthlay," Vic said firmly.

"Hyzen—what? Is that a joke?!"

"Not a joke. That's her name. *Watership Down* is my all-time favourite film. Hyzenthlay has always been my favourite rabbit in it. I always knew I would call her Hyzenthlay."

"You are naming your daughter after a rabbit?" Alex laughed and it hurt. "Only you, Vic, only you!"

K<small>ING</small> G<small>EORGE DIED</small> at the palace three days later with his closest staff next to him. On that same day, Alex and Erin got to hold their babies for the first time, still with monitors attached to them. The King's head of security, Rob Greene, came to the hospital to inform Alex straight away.

"Ma'am. I'm so sorry to have to tell you this, but your father died about half an hour ago. It was peaceful. He was in his own bed."

Alex felt everything and nothing all at once. Erin put her arm around her protectively. Alex knew this was bigger than the loss of her father. This was bigger than anything. This was the moment where she grew into her new role. She felt herself growing and strengthening.

"Ma'am. You are now the Queen. Long live Queen Alexandra." He nodded his respect.

"Do you need anything?" he asked.

Alex could think of a list a mile long. She needed to know how to be a Queen. She needed teaching. She needed to learn so much. But it could wait.

"No. Thank you, Rob. Thank you for informing me. That will be all."

He bowed to her. "Ma'am. You have my service for as long as I am capable of giving it. It will be an honour to serve you." He left the room.

"I'm so sorry, Lex," Erin said.

"It's okay." Alex felt like part of her grief was already done. "This is the beginning of the future now. Our little family. You, me, Princess Matilda, Prince Frank and Princess Florence."

"You are the Queen now. How do you feel about that, Queen Alexandra?"

"Kind of terrified. But it also feels kind of right. I have prepared my whole life for this moment. I cannot let some dangerous traitor like Arthur take the throne, it has to be me. I'm going to use it to fight for good and to do good things."

Alex had Florence on her chest against her skin. She could feel the heat of her tiny body and Alex could almost feel her heartbeat.

Erin smiled at her. "I'm so very proud of you, Mrs. Kennedy."

THE END

HER ROYAL BODYGUARD
BOOK 5

Don't miss the next instalment of the Her Royal Bodyguard Series.

You can order at the following link:
getbook.at/HRB5

Thank you so very much for reading this book. I really hope you enjoy reading these characters as much as I love writing them. I am overwhelmed with all the supportive and awesome messages and reviews. Thank you so much for buying my books and supporting an indie author. My girlfriend, dogs, cats and tortoise are very grateful too!

ALSO BY MARGAUX FOX

You can get a copy of the FREE book Play With
Me by signing up to my mailing list at the
following link and keep up with everything I am
doing.

Click on the following link or type into your
web browser to claim your free copy and join
my mailing list: https://BookHip.com/NGSVJP

"A beautiful erotic summer romance that is almost dreamlike and intimate in its delivery"

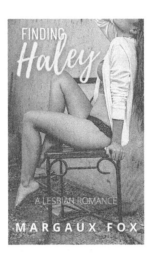

Pick up a copy of my hugely popular sunshine romance Finding Haley with the following link getbook.at/Haley

"An incredibly written tale about two amazing women and their illicit love that is so wrong, but

oh, so right. Lily is astounding and intriguing in every way."

Pick up a copy of my hugely popular romance Lily's World where a Detective falls for a Criminal Mastermind she is supposed to be investigating at the following link getbook.at/Lilysworld

If you missed it earlier, order Her Royal Bodyguard Book 5 at the following link getbook.at/HRB5

Thank you again for reading. I'm eternally grateful for your support in buying my books.

Do follow me on social media @lovefrommargaux or check out my website www.lovefrommargaux.com

Printed in Great Britain
by Amazon